Animal stories for 7 year olds

Helen Paiba was one of the most committed, knowledgeable and acclaimed children's booksellers in Britain. For more than twenty years she owned and ran the Children's Bookshop in Muswell Hill, London, which under her guidance gained a superb reputation for its range of children's books and for the advice available to its customers.

Helen was also involved with the Booksellers Association for many years and served on both its Children's Bookselling Group and the Trade Practices Committee.

In 1995 she was given honorary life membership of the Booksellers Association of Great Britain and Ireland in recognition of her outstanding services to the association and to the book trade. In the same year the Children's Book Circle (sponsored by Books for Children) honoured her with the Eleanor Farjeon Award, given for distinguished service to the world of chi...

Books in this series

Animal Stories for 5 Year Olds
Animal Stories for 6 Year Olds
Animal Stories for 7 Year Olds

Bedtime Stories for 5 Year Olds
Bedtime Stories for 6 Year Olds

Funny Stories for 5 Year Olds
Funny Stories for 6 Year Olds
Funny Stories for 7 Year Olds
Funny Stories for 8 Year Olds

Magical Stories for 5 Year Olds
Magical Stories for 6 Year Olds

Scary Stories for 7 Year Olds

Animal stories

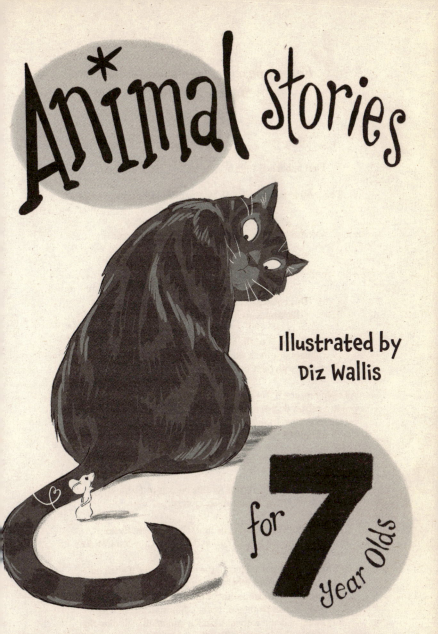

Illustrated by
Diz Wallis

for **7** year olds

Chosen by Helen Paiba

MACMILLAN CHILDREN'S BOOKS

*For my parents, who would have
enjoyed these stories. HP*

First published 1998 by Macmillan Children's Books

This edition published 2018 by Macmillan Children's Books
an imprint of Pan Macmillan
20 New Wharf Road, London N1 9RR
Associated companies throughout the world
www.panmacmillan.com

ISBN 978-1-5098-8195-6

1 3 5 7 9 8 6 4 2

A CIP catalogue record for this book is available from
the British Library.

Typeset by SX Composing DTP, Rayleigh, Essex
Printed and bound by CPI Group (UK) Ltd, Croydon CR0 4YY

Contents

A Narrow Squeak

Dick King-Smith

"Do you realize," said Ethel, "that tomorrow is our Silver Wedding Day?"

"So soon?" said Hedley in a surprised voice. "How the time flies! Why, it seems but yesterday that we were married."

"Well, it isn't," said Ethel sharply. "You only have to look at me to see that."

Hedley looked at her.

She seems to have put on a great deal of weight, he thought. Not that she isn't still by far the most beautiful mouse in the world, of course, but there's a lot more of her now.

"You have certainly grown," he said tactfully.

"Grown?" snapped Ethel. "And whose fault

1

is that, pray? Anyone would think you didn't know why I'm blown out like a balloon. Goodness knows what sort of father you will make."

"A father?" said Hedley. "You mean . . . ?"

"Any time now," said Ethel. "And I'm starving hungry, Hedley. Fetch us something nice to eat, do. I could just fancy something savoury."

She sighed deeply as her husband hurried away. Was there ever such a mouse, she said to herself. *So* handsome, but so *thick*. Let's hope he doesn't walk straight down the cat's throat. I wouldn't put it past him, and then there won't be any Silver Wedding.

A mouse's life is, of course, a short one, fraught with hazards. For those that survive their childhood, Death looms in many shapes and forms, among them the cat, the poison bait and the trap, and mice have learned to commemorate anniversaries in good time. "Better early than never" is a favourite mouse proverb, and Ethel and Hedley's Silver Wedding was to be celebrated twenty-five days after their marriage.

If they were lucky, they would go on to a Pearl, a Ruby, a Golden, and, should they be spared to enjoy roughly two months of wedded bliss, to a Diamond Wedding Anniversary. Beyond that, no sensible mouse cared to think.

If only Hedley was more sensible, Ethel thought as she lay, uncomfortably on account of the pressure within her, in her nest. Not that he isn't still by far the most beautiful mouse in the world, of course, but he's so accident-prone.

Hardly a day passed when Ethel did not hear, somewhere about the house, a thin cry of alarm, indicating that Hedley had just had a narrow squeak.

He goes about in a dream, she said to herself. He doesn't *think*. Surely other mice didn't stand in the path of vacuum cleaners, or explore inside tumble-driers, or come close to drowning in a bowl of cat's milk?

In fact, Hedley was thinking quite hard as he emerged from the hole in the skirting board that was the entrance to their home, and prepared to make his way across the kitchen floor.

"A father!" he murmured happily to himself. "I am to be a father! And soon! How many children will there be, I wonder? How many will be boys, how many girls? And what shall we call them? What fun it will be, choosing the names!"

This was what Ethel had meant when she said that Hedley did not think. Her thoughts were very practical and filled with common sense, and she was quick to make up her mind. By contrast, Hedley was a daydreamer and much inclined to be absent-minded when, as now, he was following up an idea.

He had just decided to call his eldest son Granville after a favourite uncle, when he bumped into something soft and furry, something that smelt, now that he came to think of it, distinctly unpleasant.

The cat, fast asleep in front of the Aga cooker, did not wake, but it twitched its tail.

With a shrill cry, Hedley ran for cover. The larder door was ajar, and he slipped in and hid behind a packet of Corn Flakes.

The noise he had made reached Ethel's ears, and filled her mind, as so often over the previous twenty-four days, with thoughts of widowhood. It also woke the cat, who rose, stretched and padded towards the larder.

"Not in there, puss!" said its owner, coming into her kitchen, and she shut the larder door.

Hedley was a prisoner.

For some time he crouched motionless. As happened after such frights, his mind was a blank. But gradually his thoughts returned to those unborn children. The eldest girl, now – what was she to be called?

After a while Hedley decided upon Dulcibel, his grandmother's name. But then suppose Ethel did not agree? Thinking of Ethel reminded him of her last words. "Fetch us something nice to eat, do," she had said. "I could just fancy something savoury."

Hedley raised his snout and sniffed.

This little room, in which he had never been before, certainly smelt of all kinds of food, and this reminded him that he was himself a bit peckish. He began to explore the larder, climbing up on to its shelves and running about to see what he could find. I'll have a snack, he said to himself, to keep me going, and then I'll find something really nice to take back to Ethel.

Much of the food in the larder was in cans or packets, but Hedley found a slab of fruit cake and some butter in a dish and a plate of cold chips. At last, feeling full, he hid behind a row of tins and settled down for a nap.

Meanwhile, back at the nest, Ethel was growing increasingly uneasy. He must have had his chips, she thought, and our children will be born fatherless. She was hungry, she was uncomfortable, and she was more and more worried that Hedley had not returned.

"Oh Hedley, how I shall miss you!" she breathed. "*So* handsome, but so *thick*."

While Hedley was sleeping off his huge meal, the larder door was opened.

"Just look at this cake!" a woman's voice said. "And these leftover chips! And the butter – little footmarks all over it! We've got mice."

"Put the cat in there," said a man's voice.

"Can't do that or it'll be helping itself too."

"Well, set a trap then. And put some poison down."

And a little later, the larder door was closed again.

Hedley slept the whole night through. He dreamed of happy times to come. In his dream, his handsome sons and his beautiful daughters had grown old enough to leave the nest, and he was taking them on a conducted tour of the house. Then boldly he led them all, Granville and Dulcibel and the rest, and their mother too, through the cat-flap and out into the garden. "For we will picnic," he said to them, "in the strawberry bed. The fruit is ripe and the weather exceedingly pleasant."

"Oh Papa!" the children cried. "What fun that will be!"

"But are you not afraid of the cat, Hedley dear?" said Ethel nervously.

"Ethel, Ethel," said Hedley. "When have you ever known me afraid of anything?" and the children chorused, "Oh, brave Papa!" . . .

He woke from his dream with a number of other possible names for the impending family in mind – Eugene, Tallulah, Hereward and Morwenna were four that he particularly fancied – when he suddenly remembered with a sharp pang of guilt that Ethel was still unfed.

I shall get the rough edge of her tongue, he thought, and he looked about for a tasty item of food, small enough for him to carry.

He climbed down to a lower shelf and found something which had not, he was sure, been there before.

It was a saucer containing a number of little blue pellets, and beside it there was an open packet. Had Hedley been able to read, he would have seen that on the packet was written:

*Mouse Poison, Keep Away From
Domestic Animals*

As it was, thinking how unusual and attractive the blue pellets looked, he took a mouthful of them. She'll love these, he

9

thought, such a pretty colour, and he ran down to the floor of the larder only to find the door shut. Bother, thought Hedley, How am I to get out of this place?

He was considering this problem in a half-hearted way, for part of his mind was still occupied with names – would Annabel be better than Morwenna? – when his nose caught a most exciting smell. It was cheese, a little square lump of it, conveniently placed on a low shelf.

The cheese was in fact on a little wooden platform, an odd-looking thing that had a metal arm and a spring attached to it, but Hedley, busy deciding that after all he preferred Morwenna, did not stop to think about this. It's Ethel's favourite food, he said to himself, and just the right size for me to carry back, and he spat out the little blue pellets and ran to grab the cheese.

Whether it was his speed or whether the trap had not been lightly enough set, Hedley got away with it.

SNAP! went the trap, missing him (though not by a whisker for it cut off three of them),

10

and Hedley gave, through his mouthful of cheese, a muffled squeak of fright.

"Listen!" said the woman's voice, and "You got him!" said the man's, and the larder door was opened.

For once Hedley did not daydream. He streaked across the kitchen floor and into his hole, the lump of cheese clenched in his jaws.

Ethel regarded him silently from the nest.

Hedley dropped his burden before her.

"Sorry I'm late," he panted. "I got held up. Here, it's Farmhouse Cheddar, your favourite. How have you been?"

"Busy," said Ethel shortly.

"Busy?" said Hedley.

"Yes," said Ethel.

She attacked the cheese hungrily, while Hedley lay and got his breath back. Funny, he thought, she looks slimmer than she did yesterday. As slim, in fact, as the day we met, and what a meeting that was! I remember it as though it were yesterday . . .

"Hedley!" said Ethel now, licking her lips

11

as she finished the cheese. "You do know what day it is, don't you?"

"Wednesday, I think," said Hedley. "Or it may be Thursday. I'm not sure."

"Hedley," said Ethel. "It is our Silver Wedding Day."

"Oh!" cried Hedley. "I quite forgot."

Typical, thought Ethel. He'd forget his head if it wasn't screwed on.

"I have a present for you," she said, and she rose and stood aside from the nest.

In the middle of a comfortable, warm bed, made out of flock from a chair lining, and feathers from an eiderdown, and a mass of newspaper scraps, lay six fat, pink, naked babies.

"Three boys and three girls," she said. "Neat, eh?"

Oh! thought Hedley. What could be neater! Granville and Dulcibel, Eugene and Tallulah, and Hereward and Morwenna.

"Oh, Ethel dearest," he said. "I have no present for you but my love."

At these words Ethel's annoyance melted away. What a fine-looking mouse he still is, she thought, not a grey hair on him. In fact, he looks no older than he did at our wedding, twenty-five long days ago.

Hedley sat in a daze, gazing at the babies.

Then he said, "Oh Ethel! To think that you did this all on your own! You're so *clever*!"

And you're so *thick*, thought Ethel fondly, but out loud she said, "Oh Hedley, you are *so* handsome!"

A Hat for Crumpet

Barbee Oliver Carleton

Crumpet was a big friendly trolley-horse. "Maybe I shouldn't say so," declared Crumpet. "But I suppose I'm the biggest, friendliest trolley-horse in all New York!"

Crumpet was right. Wherever she went, clippity clop, East Side, West Side, all around the town, people looked twice at Crumpet. Even the Mayor.

"And I suppose," thought Crumpet happily, "that Bill Bailey is the smartest-looking driver anywhere in the world."

Sure enough. Bill Bailey sat high and handsome on the driver's seat behind Crumpet. He tipped his hat to everyone as smartly as you please.

"Without a doubt," went on Crumpet,

looking over her shoulder, "our trolley is the prettiest little trolley you ever did see."

And it was, indeed. Golden squiggles all over the sides. Scallops on the top. "And the nicest people in New York," Crumpet decided, "sitting on the red plush seats." The mothers in their neat straw hats. The fathers in their bowler hats. The dearest and cleanest children in the world. And one fine spring morning, the Mayor himself!

"Top of the morning, Bill Bailey!" he boomed. "And what's an elegant horse like Crumpet doing without a hat? Every trolley-horse in New York has a hat!"

Elegant! The Mayor called her *elegant*! Pointing her toes, Crumpet trotted off so smartly that all the nice passengers held on to their hats to avoid losing them.

"Sure, Your Honour," laughed Bill Bailey. "I'll get her a hat for Easter."

All the way down Fifth Avenue, Crumpet peered into the hat shops. She wondered which hat Bill Bailey would buy. "Maybe," she thought, "it will be that sailor hat with the ribbons down the back. Or maybe," whispered Crumpet, "one of those wide, beautiful, elegant hats with roses around the brim!" At the very thought, Crumpet did a two-step all the way to City Hall.

That night Crumpet dreamed about hats – all sorts of hats. And every one of them was beautiful and fancy.

Next morning, in came Bill Bailey with Crumpet's breakfast. And something else.

"Here you are, Crumpet!" he sang. "Here's the comfiest, droopiest old hat anywhere in town! Found it on the dump!" And Bill Bailey, because he loved Crumpet, carefully cut two large holes for Crumpet's ears. He put the hat on Crumpet's head. "Very smart!" said Bill Bailey. Then off they started up the Avenue.

Poor Crumpet. Maybe, if she tiptoed very softly . . . and hung her head very low . . . maybe nobody would notice . . .

"What's the matter with Crumpet?" everybody asked in surprise.

"I wish I knew," worried Bill Bailey.

"I hate to say it," said the Mayor, "but an elegant trolley like this trolley needs an elegant horse to pull it."

All the nice passengers stared at Crumpet, dragging her feet up ahead. "What's the matter with Crumpet?" they asked one another.

But the children, who loved Crumpet very much, knew exactly what was the matter. They whispered to Bill Bailey. Bill Bailey said, "Well, what do you know!" Then, "Maybe you're right!" And finally, "A splendid idea!"

Crumpet, with her head hanging down by her knees and the old hat drooping over her eyes, heard the whispers. Then she heard the secret clinking of lots of coins. And then, right in front of a hat shop, she heard the CLANG-CLANG of the trolley-bell. Crumpet stopped. Some passengers got off. Crumpet's heart was so heavy that she didn't even wonder what Bill Bailey was waiting for. She squeezed her eyes tight shut to hold back the tears.

Then a voice said softly, "Crumpet, this is for you."

Crumpet lifted her head. There beside her were the children, taking something out of a box. A something that was wide and beautiful and elegant! It was blooming with roses and streaming with streamers! Off came the comfy old hat. On went the beautiful new one. Gently, the children tied the streamers under Crumpet's chin.

"Happy Easter, Crumpet!" they smiled. Then they hopped back on to the trolley.

CLANG-CLANG-CLANG! went the bell. Up came Crumpet's head in the elegant hat. She pointed her toes daintily. Then, with her nose held high and her roses bobbing and her streamers flying, off down the avenue she trotted.

All the way along the route, Crumpet sang to herself: *"Clippity-clop! twiddle-dee-dee! This is just the hat for a horse like me!"*

The Lion and the Hare

A Story from Botswana

Retold by Michael Rosen

Once upon a time, many years ago, Tau the lion met Mmutla the hare.

Mmutla thought to himself, as he saw Tau coming towards him, here comes the king of the beasts, I will try to trick him.

So Mmutla said to the lion, "Good morning, Your Majesty, you must be very lonely and sad, living on your own. May I come and live with you?"

Tau the lion grunted and looked hard at the hare but he didn't say anything.

So Mmutla the hare continued, "Surely you don't like doing all your own cooking, cleaning and washing? Let me come and do all your work. Let me come and clean for you, let me come and wash for you. I could do all your hard work. You are much too important to do everything for yourself."

The lion thought for a moment, then he said, "It would be nice to have someone else to do all my cooking and cleaning and washing. And people say that hares are so good at housework. Mmmm, it's very tempting . . . I tell you what, I will find the food, you can cook it and wash up afterwards. You can keep my home tidy and do all the hard work. Good, I like it. And don't try and trick me – understand?"

"Would I?" said the hare. "Would I try and trick you? Perish the thought. You've made a good bargain – you fetch the food, I cook it. And believe me, I'm not afraid of hard work."

So Tau the lion showed the hare where he had his home.

Mmutla the hare pretended to be shocked.

"But this won't do for the king of the beasts. It's much too uncomfortable. We must build a fine comfortable house."

"Very good idea," said the lion. I've

certainly got a servant with the right ideas here, he thought. "Let's start at once."

The lion and the hare started work on the new house straight away. They worked non-stop for days. Hare fetched and carried and lifted hour after hour. Tau the lion just could not believe his luck. Here was a real servant.

They were nearly finished when Mmutla the hare said, "Look, I'm really hungry. Why don't we sit down and have something to eat?"

"No!" said the lion. "I decide what happens around here. I am the master and you are the servant. We'll eat when we've finished. The last job to do is putting the roof on. When that's done, we'll eat. Now no more moaning, and get on with it or you'll have nothing at all."

So they set to, putting the roof on. Tau the lion held the grass in place and Mmutla the hare threaded the great needle in and out of the grass, tying it to the beams. Then, as quick as lightning, the hare slipped a loop of the thread over the lion's front paw. Then, just as quickly again, he slipped a loop over the lion's other front paw. Tau was tied to the roof of the hut. He couldn't move. He struggled, he roared. He roared, he struggled, but it was no use.

Mmutla the hare just laughed.

"Now what was it you were saying about me not having my dinner till we had finished? Well, I tell you what – I'll have my dinner now. I'm so sorry you can't join me."

So while the lion struggled and wriggled, Mmutla the hare finished all the food.

But lions are very strong and it wasn't long before the thread broke and Tau was free. He jumped down and chased the hare. You can be sure, Mmutla was scared, really scared. He ran like he had never run before. He ran till he saw a hole in the ground and bolted down it – just in time. But Tau thrust his great paw down the hole and grabbed hold of Mmutla's leg. Mmutla tried digging his claws into the ground but slowly Tau the lion was dragging him out of the hole. What am I going to do? thought the hare.

Then he shouted out as loud as he could, "You'll never get me out. That's not my leg you've got hold of there. It's the root of the tree. You might pull the tree down, but you won't get me, you big mutt."

Tau let go of Mmutla's leg and made a grab for anything else he could feel. This time it *was* the root of the tree.

"Ah," shouted Mmutla, "right, you've got my leg now. I should never have told you that."

So Tau heaved and pulled on the root while the hare hurried on down deep into the hole. The hole ran along for a good way and then came up about twenty metres from where Tau the lion was still tugging on the tree root.

Up popped Mmutla the hare. "Cooee, you old fool. Thanks for letting me go. What a friend you are."

And off he ran, with the lion pounding along behind him.

It wasn't long before Tau caught up with the hare, right on the banks of a deep river. I must get across here, whatever else happens, thought Mmutla.

Tau pounced on him and held him in his great paws.

"Oh mighty one," sobbed Mmutla. "Oh, you

don't know how sorry I am. I am truly sorry for what I have done. It was a mean trick and it will never happen again. Look, you can do anything that you want with me. Kill me, eat me, feed me to the birds, but whatever you do, keep me away from my worst enemy. He lives on the other side of the river. Over there. Please, I beg of you, don't let him get his hands on me or I'll die the most agonizing death the world has ever seen."

Tau the lion laughed, "Ah ha-hah! I'll make you sorry all right. I'll make you sorry that you tried to trick the king of the beasts. I don't think I can come up with a horrible enough way for you to die, but your enemy over there seems to have the right idea. I *will* give you to him, no matter what you say."

At that, Tau the lion flung Mmutla as hard as he could over the river.

When he landed on the other side, Mmutla called back to the lion, "Thanks. You're a real friend. I haven't got any enemies over here, you dumb dolt. All you've just done is help me get away from *you*."

And off he ran.

Now Tau was angry. Actually he wasn't just angry, he was furious. He could have roared the forest down if he had tried. He caught sight of a log floating down the river and he leapt on to it. Meanwhile Mmutla was running along thinking he was safe, but the log was floating faster and faster down the river, after Mmutla. It wasn't long before the log got close enough to the river bank for the lion to leap from it and on to the bank. And now he hurtled after the hare.

Mmutla had slowed down to a jog and was looking about himself thinking how clever he had been. Tau the lion caught sight of him, slowed down, crouched, and inched nearer and nearer. Then with one great bound, he leapt out of the bushes right on to the hare. Mmutla was well and truly caught.

Now I'm done for, thought Mmutla. This is the end.

But even as he was thinking this he was looking around him, trying to find some way out.

"Now you've caught me once and for all, oh great one. These are my last moments on earth. And I deserve to be eaten. I only say this, don't forget to say your prayers and thank God for what you are about to eat."

Quite right, thought Tau, I should thank God. And he closed his eyes to pray. The moment he did, Mmutla the hare grabbed a stone and hurled it into a bees' nest he had noticed in the tree above them. The bees went crazy, and swarmed around looking for who had disturbed them.

Mmutla made off like the wind, but Tau the

lion sat there with his eyes shut thanking God with all his might. Down came the bees and went for him. They stung every bit of him they could find and when they couldn't find any more bits to sting, they stung the bits all over again. It was weeks before he was well enough to think about chasing Mmutla again.

But now he had the memory of all that pain to spur him on.

"I'll catch that revolting little hare, if it's the last thing I ever do. I don't mind how long I have to wait, but I'll get him."

His chance came not long after. He caught sight of Mmutla asleep by some rocks. He crept nearer and nearer . . . and jumped. But Mmutla wasn't asleep, he was just resting with one eye open on the look-out for danger. Just when Tau was in mid-air, flying towards him, Mmutla the hare leapt out from under the lion. The lion landed on the ground with a thud, but Mmutla didn't run off. He leapt at the rocks.

"Quick! Quick!" he shouted. "I've just saved your life. Didn't you see it? When you jumped just then, you disturbed the rocks. If I hadn't leapt up here to hold that one back, you'd've been crushed to death by it."

"Wow," said Tau the lion. "Thanks, thanks a lot."

"Don't just stand there thanking me," said the hare. "Come over here and help me. You're much stronger than I am. Get your shoulder behind this and you'll be safe."

Up jumped Tau and wedged his body under the rock and heaved.

"Whatever you do now," said Mmutla the hare, "don't let go or you'll be crushed to death. You're doing a great job there. Stick at it. I'll rush off and get some help." At that, Mmutla patted the lion on the head and off he ran as fast as he could.

Tau strained and heaved against that rock for days before he realized that he had been tricked. And when he did he felt very, very silly. Mmutla, by now, was a long, long way away and Tau never saw him again.

Jeffy and Miss Amity

Ursula Moray Williams

Nobody, seeing Miss Amity and her little cat walking down the street to the library on a Saturday morning, would have believed that Miss Amity was a burglar.

She was so neat and tidy and old . . . so cheerful, and so polite. One imagined that she had worn that little black hat all her life, also the black knitted gloves, the dress with the lace-edged collar and the blue butterfly brooch pinned upon it, which must surely have been given to her on her birthday many years ago. Her eyes behind the old-fashioned spectacles flashed from one side of the street to the other, greeting her friends:

"Good morning Mrs Davis! Good morning Nurse Black! Good morning Mr Green!

Perhaps the weather will clear up later? Now whatever will the Government think of next?"

Her shopping bag was full, like every other shopping bag, with packets of washing-powder, library books, fruit, postage stamps, and of cat-food for Jeffy her cat, but underneath the cat-food it was really a burglar bag, full of tools like jemmies and other house-breaking implements. Miss Amity just loved carrying them around with her.

Her little cat Jeffy had no idea of his mistress's wicked employment. He loved her very dearly and he called her Missammitty. She had adopted him when he was a kitten.

There are usually too many kittens in the world, which is very sad, but true, and Jeffy's excellent little mother, Miss Brown, was one of those cats who were always having too many kittens. Jeffy was one of them, and when she knew that she would not be able to keep him, Miss Brown picked him up and dropped him on the doorstep of the kindest old lady she knew, and that old lady was Miss Amity.

Before she left him there his mother whispered into his ear all the maxims of good training she would normally spread over the first few months of his life.

"Always be clean and tidy!" she told him, giving him a final spit and polish round the ears. "Always be honest! Never take what does not belong to you . . . not once! . . . *not ever!* Think before you act, and wash before you think!"

Then she was gone, and Jeffy's head which had been so warm and comfortable under her licking tongue began to feel very cold indeed.

Miss Amity found him crying, and took him into her home and into her heart, just as his mother had hoped she would. She fed him and brought him up and promised him a happy home for ever and ever. Jeffy thought she was the best mistress in the world; he had no idea that she was really a burglar.

Not until one night when he caught her climbing in through the window, in disguise.

Jeffy woke up with a start in the darkness. He slept inside a cupboard, curled up in Miss

Amity's work-basket, and usually she shut the cupboard door when she went upstairs.

But on this particular night the cupboard door was open, just a crack, and the noise that woke Jeffy was the burglar bag being dropped on the floor as Miss Amity climbed in through the kitchen window.

Jeffy sat bolt upright in the work-basket. He was pricked by a couple of pins, so he jumped lightly on to the floor inside the cupboard.

"Missammitty! Is that you, Missammitty?" he called out in the darkness. Instantly there was perfect silence. Jeffy listened, and while he listened he washed, to fill in the time, and while he washed he heard somebody moving very quietly across the kitchen floor.

Quick as a flash Jeffy was round the corner of the door, and there, crawling across the linoleum, which was clearly lit up by the lamps in the street outside, was a burglar!

The burglar wore a black slouch hat and dark spectacles. He had long black moustaches dripping down by his chin, and he carried a burglar bag.

Jeffy let out a screech for his mistress that must have woken all the cats in the street and some of their owners as well.

"Missammitty! Oh Missammitty! Come quickly!" He was about to follow it with: "Thieves! Robbers! Burglars! Police! Police! Police!" when the burglar leapt to his feet and banged the window shut.

"You stupid cat! Don't you know me?" scolded the burglar, tearing off the cap, the glasses and the moustache, and there *was* Miss Amity!

Jeffy was so upset that she had to take off all the rest of her burglar clothes and make a cup of tea, so that he could have some condensed milk to settle him down.

"Well now, Jeffy!" she said when he had stopped shaking. "What's wrong with my being a burglar, anyhow?"

"What's inside the bag?" Jeffy faltered, with spatters of condensed milk trembling on his chin.

"Nothing much!" said Miss Amity lightly.

"Really nothing much? Really *nothing*? Or how much?" Jeffy demanded.

"*Nothing* much!" said Miss Amity firmly.

"But how *much* nothing much?" Jeffy persisted.

"Oh well, just one tiny little diamond ring!" said Miss Amity defiantly.

Jeffy pounced on the bag, and drew out the ring with his paw. It was quite true; it was the only object inside the bag except the burgling tools.

"From the Towers," said Miss Amity with satisfaction. "She's got lots and lots more like it, and it was such lovely fun climbing up the drainpipe!"

"It's *thieving*!" said Jeffy, horrified. "It's wicked! It's awful! I just don't know what my mother would say if she knew I'd come to live with a person that stole things."

Miss Amity stared.

"Do you mean you think it's wrong of me, Jeffy?" she said.

"Of course it's wrong," said Jeffy. "My mother told me: Never never take anything that doesn't belong to you. Not once. Not ever. I can't just go on living with a person like that. My mother wouldn't like it at all."

"Oh Jeffy dear, I'll put it back! I'll put it back!" Miss Amity said. "I only did it for fun! I didn't mean to keep it!"

"*When* will you put it back?" Jeffy asked.

"This very minute," said Miss Amity brightly beginning to put on her disguise again, and snatching the ring out of Jeffy's paw.

But already the early morning was breaking on the world outside. Whistles were shrilling, and police cars came dashing up the street on their way to the Towers.

"There!" Jeffy said. "It's no good. They've found out everything already. You can't go back now or you'll be caught." Immediately he found he wanted to protect Miss Amity.

"Never mind," she said bravely. "I'll face them. I'll tell the truth. I'll explain I only did it for fun. I'll say it was just a game and I was going to put it back the next morning."

"You burgled," said Jeffy. "They'll punish you just the same."

"But surely not if I say I'm sorry?" said Miss Amity, crestfallen. "*You* believe me, don't you, Jeffy?"

"I'm not a policeman," said Jeffy. "So I think the best thing to do is to put it back myself."

"Oh what a *good* idea! What a clever little cat you are!" said Miss Amity. "Would you like to borrow my whiskers and my cap and my gloves and my burglar bag? They may be a little big for you my dear!"

"I don't want any of them," said Jeffy severely. "Just give me the ring."

"Oh well," said Miss Amity, "I'll have some warm milk ready for you when you come in."

It was almost too simple, and afterwards Jeffy wished he could have had more of a narrow escape to describe to Miss Amity as a warning, when it was all over.

For there was nobody in the streets, and the driveway of the Towers was floodlit by the beams from police cars. Inside the house he could see lights blazing, and more policemen gathered round the library table, taking notes. The front door was guarded by a huge policeman standing at attention.

Jeffy just went up to him and yowled and yowled round his legs, till the policeman took pity on him, opened the door, and let him inside.

"Poor old pusskins! Did she get shut out then? Well, well, that's what you get for going out on the tiles. Serves you right, Puss! Serves you right!"

Jeffy trotted across the empty hall to the staircase and spat the ring into a corner of the stairs. Then he went to the back of the house and yowled and yowled until another policeman let him out again.

"Poor old pussycat! Got a rendezvous? Mustn't keep Miss Tabitha waiting!"

He was back in his own house in ten minutes' time. Miss Amity had not even begun to warm the milk.

"Well," she said, placidly filling the saucepan. "There's nothing to it, is there?" and even as she spoke the police cars began to come back down the street, quite quietly, in the direction of the police station. It was obvious that the diamond ring had been found very quickly and everyone thought it had all been a false alarm.

But Jeffy refused to drink any milk, and

went to bed in a temper. He would hardly speak to Miss Amity in the morning.

"Jeffy, Jeffy! How can you be so unkind to your missis?" Miss Amity coaxed him, nearly in tears.

"You're a burglar," said Jeffy flatly. "And my mother said . . ."

"Oh I know, I know. But I *was* a burglar. I'm not now!" said Miss Amity happily. "And you are a very clever, well-brought-up little cat. Your mother would be proud of you. Just think, Jeffy, I might be eating my cornflakes in prison this morning if it wasn't for you."

"Yes," agreed Jeffy, drinking his milk at last.

"So we'll just forget all about it, shall we, Jeffy?" coaxed Miss Amity. "And we'll be best friends again, and go down to the grocer to fetch some tins of Catsprat. I know you like Catsprat, Jeffy. Catsprat's for clever cats!"

Jeffy could not keep up his ill-temper for long, and he was flattered by Miss Amity's praise. He hoped she had learnt her lesson, for he had had a nasty shock.

He tried to prop open the cupboard door,

just a chink, at night, but Miss Amity always closed it firmly when she went to bed. Then he took to sleeping in the burglar bag. When Miss Amity tried to remove him to put him in the cupboard he clung on tightly, dragging up all the burglar things from the bottom, so that the false beard dangled from his feet and the cap fell out onto the carpet.

"Look what you've done!" Miss Amity scolded, picking them up. "And I might never have thought of them again if you hadn't reminded me!"

Jeffy felt as guilty as if he had personally led her into temptation. But all he said was: "You'd better not!"

There were festivities in the town when the new Mayor was elected. There was to be a grand tea for the schoolchildren, and another for the Town Council, when the old Mayor would hand over his chain of office to the new one.

Jeffy and Miss Amity watched the preparations going on outside the Town Hall when they changed their books at the library.

A big marquee had been put up in the public gardens, and long trestle tables were set up in it for the schoolchildren, with a big table at the end for the Mayor and Town Council to sit at.

On the morning of the party Miss Amity said she would just slip out to the shops to get a little bit of fish for their dinner, and afterwards she would take Jeffy to see the procession that would go through the town before the Mayor was elected and everybody went into tea.

Jeffy was sitting on the window sill in the sunshine when Miss Amity returned. She came flying down the street, and indeed she was puffing as if she had done quite a lot of running. The shopping bag, when she put it down, sounded heavy.

There was something much heavier than fish in Miss Amity's shopping bag.

"What have you got in that bag, Miss-ammitty?" said Jeffy suspiciously.

"Nothing!" said Miss Amity with spirit.

"Do you mean nothing? Or nothing to do with me?" asked Jeffy.

42

"Nothing to do with you!" snapped Miss Amity.

"Ha!" said Jeffy. "And perhaps that means nothing to do with you either! Am I right, Missammitty?"

"Oh well, if you put it that way . . . yes!" said Miss Amity looking coy, and giggling a little.

"Have you been burgling again?" Jeffy asked her.

"Why no, Jeffy, no! Of course I wouldn't! Burgling is done at night in burglar's clothes with jemmies and things. Do I look as if I had been burgling?" said Miss Amity with indignation.

"Well, stealing, then! Robbery! Daylight robbery?" suggested Jeffy.

Miss Amity cast down her eyes and tried to shuffle the shopping bag behind her skirts. "Well, just a little bit," she admitted.

Jeffy lost his temper with her.

"This time it's too much! I'm going to leave you!" he expostulated.

"Oh Jeffy, Jeffy!" Miss Amity cried, taking off her gloves and flinging them to the floor. "I didn't mean it! I didn't mean it! I didn't really! I do want to be honest and live a good life like your mother told you to do! Oh what shall I do? What shall I do?"

"What did you take this time?" Jeffy asked crossly.

"Not much," said Miss Amity slyly, still trying to keep the bag from Jeffy's view.

"Well, what?"

"Only two little sandwiches!"

"And?"

"And two tomatoes . . ."

"*And . . .*"

"And some mustard'n cress . . ."

"AND . . . ?"

"And the Mayor's chain of office!" wept Miss Amity, bursting into tears and hurling a handful of golden metal across the room with such force that it cracked the sink.

"Now look what you've done," cried Jeffy. "When we wash up all the water will go on the floor. Oh why, why, why do you do such things, Missammitty?"

"I don't know," wept Miss Amity. "I didn't mean to throw it so hard. I didn't mean it!"

"Not the sink . . . *the Mayor's chain of*

office!" said Jeffy. "And the sandwiches and the tomatoes and the mustard and cress! It's all of it pinching and stealing and wickedness, and I've told you before my mother said I wasn't to have anything to do with it. I'm off!"

"Oh, Jeffy! Jeffy!" wept Miss Amity, collapsing on top of the sandwiches with her head on her arms.

"Don't do that! You're squashing them!" Jeffy cried in alarm. "And then we won't be able to take them back."

"Oh will you really, dear Jeffy? Oh Jeffy, how good you are to poor, wicked old me!" Miss Amity cried, getting up and prancing for joy. "Then I won't have to go to prison, and we'll live happily ever after! Oh you are the very best little cat in the world, and I don't deserve you, I know I don't!"

"I may not come back to you afterwards," Jeffy said severely, sweeping the sandwiches, the tomatoes and the mustard and cress into a paper bag, and winding the Mayor's chain several times round his neck under the thick fur of his collar and chin. "My mother would have a fit if she knew I was living with a thief and a robber, and I don't like it myself one little bit."

"Don't you love me any more?" said Miss Amity, with tears now running down her chin. "You mother was quite right. I don't deserve to have a cat like you, and I must do without it. But I shall think of you all the rest of my life. Promise me just one thing before you leave me for ever. When you have taken back the sandwiches, Jeffy dear, and the tomatoes, and the mustard and cress and the Mayor's golden chain, come back and show yourself to me for just one little minute so that I can be sure that they haven't caught you and put you in prison!"

"Pah!" said Jeffy crossly. But to set her mind at rest he promised Miss Amity that he would.

Nobody took much notice of a little cat trotting through the streets with a paper bag in its mouth. They thought it had been stealing out of dustbins.

Jeffy could not run fast, because the weight of the chain wound round his neck was quite suffocating, and he found it difficult to raise his head.

Outside the town hall a queue of schoolchildren was impatiently waiting to go into the marquee where tea was set out on long tables, but inside, everyone was frantically searching for the chain of office, which seemed to have completely disappeared. They were so busy that it was easy enough for Jeffy to jump on to the table and replace the sandwiches, the tomatoes and the mustard and cress, but the heavy chain so

weighed him down that he landed with a crash among the crockery, which brought the waitresses running into the tent, joined by half a dozen waiters from the kitchen.

"Cat's after the food!" they shouted, and Jeffy was chased from one end of the table to the other, dodging glasses, plates and bowls of jelly as he ran, until, in making a great leap to escape from his pursuers he fell with a splash into an enormous bowl of fruit salad that the Mayor had specially ordered to please the children.

The caterers, the waitresses and the waiters all sprang backwards to escape the fountains of juice cascading over the table. Then they fled to the kitchen to find cloths to wipe up the mess, while Jeffy clawed for the edge of the bowl.

As he did so, the golden chain of office slipped off his wet and slippery neck into the bottom of the salad. The chief of the caterers found it there later when he emptied out the bowl in the kitchen, to replace it with fresh fruit. He thought somebody must have been playing tricks on him.

"And if it hadn't been for that perishing cat we might never have found it!" he said, carrying the chain in triumph to the Mayor.

Jeffy arrived home sticky with fruit juice and with apricot slices clinging to his fur.

Miss Amity bathed and dried him, telling him how good and clever he was.

"It's all very well," Jeffy said, giving his coat an angry licking after the bath, "but if I hadn't fallen into the fruit salad they would have caught me, and I would have been put into prison instead of you. Just because you went out stealing like a common thief."

"But I'll never do it again, dear Jeffy," Miss Amity promised, drying him with tender hands. "Not if you will stay with me and make sure that I don't, and keep reminding me what your good little mother taught you."

"Will you *promise*?" said Jeffy, feeling warm and comfortable again.

"I promise I will never be a common thief again," said Miss Amity.

"Or a burglar," Jeffy insisted.

"Or a burglar," Miss Amity promised. "Never again! Not ever!"

49

The Visit of Fudge

A.N. Wilson

The new guinea-pig was called Tobacco. He had a contented nature, he enjoyed his food and he liked Hazel. They made a very happy pair. Hazel lost that slight wistfulness which she had had when she lived on her own. She no longer scurried about so much, everlastingly on the lookout for something. She had found what she was looking for. She discovered that many of life's simple pleasures were twice as enjoyable when they were shared with an amiable companion. In the old days, if someone put an apple core into the hutch, she would have eaten it cheerfully enough. But now, as well as there being something to eat there was something to talk about.

"Anything important?" Tobacco called from the bedroom, hearing that there had been a delivery next door.

"A bit of fruit by the looks of things," said Hazel.

"Fruit, eh?"

Hazel never fully remembered *all* the fruits that there were, but Tobacco had a real knowledge of the subject. As he came out of the bedroom he said, "It could be a bit of orange peel. Then again, it could be a pear."

"Ar," said Hazel. "It could be a pear."

She was eating some of it and couldn't rightly make up her mind.

"It could be, girl," Tobacco conceded.

He had taken to calling Hazel "girl", and she seemed to like it, though she never called him "boy".

"But as it happens, this is . . ."

"It's nice," said Hazel.

"That it is," said Tobacco, sinking his teeth into the apple core. He had momentarily forgotten what this particular fruit was called, but it was very delicious.

When they had nibbled it down to almost

nothing, Tobacco shared with Hazel some of his almost-memories of the old days. He had no memory for things which had happened very recently. But there were some fascinating things lodged in his memory from three or four weeks before, when he lived with his parents in a rather over-crowded hutch. He did not *know* that they had been his parents, and when he thought of his father it was simply a half-memory of an old black and white who had talked rather a lot.

"I knew a guinea-pig once . . ." said Tobacco, remembering his father but not *knowing* that it was his father.

"Now I can't remember whether I ever did," said Hazel.

"This guinea-pig," said Tobacco, "he said the best fruit to eat was called Barn Anna. White, I believe it is."

"More like a cabbage?" asked Hazel.

"Could be."

"This here fruit was nice," said Hazel, surveying the few remnants of the apple core. "What did you say it was? My memory's terrible. Not like yours."

Tobacco went to the bars of the hutch and sniffed.

"It's a really nice day today, girl. Let's hope they put us out on the lawn."

"Oh, that would be nice," said Hazel. "I likes the lawn."

A few minutes later the children came and put the guinea-pigs in the run on the lawn. When Tobacco and Hazel ran about together on the grass, they were a joy to see. They were so happy, so playful, so carefree.

Now it so happened that on that day, the children who looked after the guinea-pigs were planning a surprise for Tobacco. The girl had told all her friends about him. Yes, Hazel was a wonderful, beautiful creature. And when she had owned just Hazel, the girl had believed that it would not have been possible to love a guinea-pig more. But after Tobacco arrived, well . . . comparisons are odious. The girl did love Tobacco very, very much indeed. He was so friendly and happy, and he chirruped when you picked him up and put him in your jumper. The girl had told her friends that Tobacco was the handsomest, the most chirruping, the friendliest and the best *boy* guinea-pig in the world.

The girl's best friend, another girl called Rona, was also very fond of guinea-pigs, and she had one whom she considered the prettiest, the most chirruping et cetera: Fudge was a special breed, known by guinea-pig experts (or, as they call themselves, Cavey Fanciers) as American Crested.

The girl who looked after Hazel and Tobacco knew that no girl guinea-pig could be nicer than Hazel. But she agreed with Rona that it would be very exciting if Fudge could have some babies. And if the prettiest, most chirruping et cetera were to mate with the handsomest, most chirruping et cetera, they would have the most et cetera *baby* guinea-pigs in the world. Some of them might even turn out to be et cetera *cresteds*, and that was an exciting thought. So the girl had agreed that Rona should bring round Fudge that Saturday morning, and that Fudge should spend the weekend in a separate hutch with Tobacco. But as with so many things which sounded like a good idea, it actually turned out badly.

"This," Tobacco was saying, "is what I'd call juicy. Real juicy grass, this."

Hazel gazed at him admiringly. He had such a way of putting things. But just then the side of the run was lifted up and a hand reached in and grabbed Tobacco in mid-sentence. He was just saying, "I knew this guinea-pig once who knew about grass . . ."

"Don't squeak, Baccy darling," said the girl. "You are going to meet Fudge."

"Oh, he *is* sweet," said Rona. "He's so nice and glossy."

"Fudge is nice, too," said the girl politely.

Tobacco stayed still in the girl's hands and quietened down. She sat on the grass and held him in her lap. He looked this way and that. This way he could see the wife, running about the run, saying, "Ar, juicy, that's the word for it." And that way, the other way, he could see some knees, clad in a pair of jeans, and some hands on which the nails were rather bitten down, and in the hands the silliest-looking guinea-pig Tobacco had ever seen in his life. It was an orange affair (not that he troubled himself about colours; as it happened he couldn't make out colours). And it had this sort of fur-hat thing on its head. Well, really! Tobacco tried to think of a word for it and selected the word *silly*.

"I mean," he said quietly to himself, "a head's a head. Just a head. You don't need to go dolling it up with a sort of *hat* effort."

"I think he chirruped then," said the girl optimistically.

"It sounded more like a whimper," said her friend Rona.

"No," said the girl firmly, "it was a definite chirrup."

"I so very much hope," said Rona, "that they'll like one another."

"It is impossible not to like Tobacco," said the girl.

"Shall we try putting them together in the hutch?" said Rona.

The girl stood up and carried Tobacco down to the garden shed where the hutches were, and Rona followed carrying Fudge. The girl opened the bedroom door of the hutch and put Tobacco inside. Tobacco felt disappointed that he had been given such a very *short* time in the run. He had been enjoying the fresh air, and the grass, and the good talk. But he contented himself with the certainty that Hazel would soon be brought to join him.

"Shall we put Fudge in the bedroom, too?" asked the girl.

"No," said Rona, "I'll put her in this living-room part of the hutch."

So this they did. And then they shut the doors, making sure that they were fastened securely. The two girls peered into the hutch. Fudge chirruped and nuzzled into Tobacco's feeding bowl.

"She loves that bran," said Rona. Then she added coyly, "I expect they want to be left on their own."

And the two girls walked out of the shed, leaving the guinea-pigs to their own devices. They went and sat on the lawn and watched Hazel munching her grass-feast in the run.

"Wouldn't it be lovely if Fudge had some babies," said Rona.

"A whole litter of crested Tobaccos," said her friend. "As glossy and friendly and sweet as Tobacco, only with little crests on their heads! If Fudge *does* have a litter of babies, would you let me have one?"

"Would your mum let you have three guinea-pigs?" asked Rona.

"Of course she wouldn't," said the girl's brother who had come out to join them. He thought it was soppy to be drooling over the little creatures in this way. He wanted someone to play French cricket with, and waved a tennis racket grandly. "Come and play a game."

"Not if you're going to be rude about Baccy," said his sister.

"I'd like to play," said Rona.

So they all went off to the nearby park to play French cricket.

Inside the hutch, Tobacco lay in his hay bed for a while, and felt sad. Then he decided that there was no point in sulking, and he had no sooner made this sensible decision than his spirits lifted. He heard some munching and scuffling next door in the living-room and he happily assumed that Hazel had been brought to join him.

"I could have done with longer on the grass, girl," he called from the bedroom.

But as he waddled out to join her, he did not hear the familiar cries of "Ar" or "That's right". Instead, to his absolute amazement, he saw Silly Hat bold as brass, standing in *their* living-room and eating *their* food.

"Get back in there if you value your life," said Fudge angrily.

"What did you say?"

"You heard."

"That's not manners," said Tobacco.

"And who are you, I should like to know."

As he spoke, all the fur stood up on his back. He felt a violent hostility to Silly Hat. He felt so angry that he would have liked to bite the silly pig.

"Warned you!" said Fudge, who ran towards Tobacco with fur on edge and teeth bared.

The fight was sharp and furious. Fudge tried to jump on Tobacco's back and bite his neck. Tobacco threw Fudge off and scratched at the enemy with his claws. Then to his great satisfaction he managed to get a good mouthful of Fudge's crest. He yanked and tugged with his teeth and succeeded in pulling out some of the fur before Fudge biffed him with a claw on the side of his head and knocked him dizzy.

"I'll teach you to pull my crown, you common little *brat*!" howled Fudge.

"Crown! Huh! Silly hat more like," said Tobacco.

He regretted saying this, because it excited in Fudge a truly murderous fury.

"No one insults the cresteds and gets away with it," hissed Fudge, through two slightly protuberant front teeth, both very sharp. "Particularly not a *thing*, like you."

Fudge pounced on poor Tobacco and knocked him over on his back. Tobacco waved his paws about and shrieked in despair; he was completely powerless. He looked up and saw the open mouth of Fudge, and two long sharp fangs coming closer and closer to his throat.

Then, just in the nick of time, the door of the hutch opened, and Mum's hand reached inside and picked up Tobacco. He was quivering with fright and he had a cut on the side of his head.

"Poor Tobacco," said Mum.

She stroked him, and kissed him and examined his cut. It was not so bad as it looked. Mum put Tobacco in the run with Hazel. Then Mum went to the garden shed once more. She took Fudge out of Tobacco and Hazel's hutch.

"Come on, Fudge," said Mum. "We'll put you in this spare hutch over here."

It just happened that Mum had been

weeding the flower bed near the garden shed. She had heard the furious squeakings of Fudge and Tobacco and had gone to see what was the matter with them. Mum did not blame either of the guinea-pigs for fighting. She was not cross with Fudge for having flown at Tobacco. She realized that it was just nature. She was just a *little* cross with the children for having gone off, leaving the guinea-pigs before checking that they were getting on well. A nasty incident had been narrowly avoided.

In the run, Tobacco was still shaking with the shock of it all.

"How you been and got that nasty cut?" asked Hazel, her mouth full of grass.

"Silly Hat done it," said Tobacco.

"What's that then?"

"You've been all right, girl, eating grass in here."

"Ar," agreed Hazel. "I've been all right."

"But they've gone and bought this terrible pig with a thing on its head like you never saw."

"What kind of a thing?"

"Well, hat's the only word for it," said Tobacco. "And a darned silly one at that."

"Mind your language," said Hazel.

"Well, silly, then, and never mind about the darned."

"That's better."

"And where do you think they've gone and put this Silly Hat creature?"

"Where?"

"In our hutch, that's where."

"What, not in *our* hutch?"

"That's right, girl."

"Another guinea-pig?"

"Like I says, with this darned – sorry – with this Silly Hat thing on its head."

"That wouldn't be right," said Hazel. "Not on its head, a hat."

And then Tobacco felt fonder of Hazel than he had ever felt before, and he went and stood so that his nose was very nearly touching her nose. And then he thought how beautiful she was – so plump and sleek and brown and glossy. And he made a noise which the girl called chirruping – but actually he was saying, "That's my girl."

They talked for ages about Silly Hat while they munched their grass. Tobacco partly talked so much about it because he couldn't stop, and partly to remind himself of what had happened in case he forgot it.

"Then it came at me," he said.

"Oh *dear*," said Hazel

"But I gave it what for," said Tobacco.

"I bet you did," said Hazel, "But you shouldn't go fighting."

Although Hazel said this, she was secretly very proud of Tobacco for defending their hutch against an intruder.

Tobacco said, "Then I says 'Don't come a step further,' I says, 'or I won't be actionable for my answers.'"

"Oh *dear!*" exclaimed Hazel.

"It came at me," said Tobacco, "but I were ready. Its teeth were bared, and it were hissing and oh, girl – the stink of the creature."

"What did you do?" asked Hazel.

"Do?" asked Tobacco. "What else could I do? I just fought it. I give as good as I got, girl."

"I'm sure," said Hazel. "But you didn't ought to have got into no fight."

"It come at me," said Tobacco, "but I knocked it sideways. Flat. That's what I knocked it. I really think if that lady hadn't have come along, Silly Hat would have been a goner."

"I'm glad you didn't . . ." Hazel hesitated. Either she could not find the word "kill" or she did not want to use it. Instead she asked, "Where are we going to live? We can't share a hutch with Silly Hat."

"We shall *protest*," said Tobacco. "If they pick us up and tries to put us in that hutch with Silly Hat, we must wriggle, we must struggle, we must shout. We must never allow them to put us in there."

When the children returned from their game, and tried to catch Tobacco and Hazel, they found it astonishingly difficult. Both the guinea-pigs ran round the run and *wouldn't* be caught. And when they were eventually caught, they squealed and squealed, demanding to be free. But it was all right. When they got back to their hutch they found that Silly Hat had been taken away. She had gone home with Rona.

"I can still smell that *thing* in here, you know, girl," said Tobacco, indignantly walking up and down the living-room.

"Oh come to bed and stop worrying."

Much later as they lay in the hay, Tobacco said quietly to Hazel. "I'm glad it's gone."

"Me too," said Hazel.

"I'm glad it's just you and me, girl."

"That would be right," said Hazel.

The whole incident caused the children embarrassment and worry. The girl had told Rona that Tobacco was so friendly. Rona had said the same thing about Fudge.

"And it would have been so wonderful if Fudge could have had Tobacco's babies," said the girl.

"Wonderful, indeed," said Mum. "It would have been a miracle."

"Why is that?" asked the girl.

"Surely you realize by now," said Mum, "that Fudge is a boy."

How the Ostrich Got his Long Neck

A story from East Africa

Phyllis Savory

Mr Ostrich was a sober-minded, serious husband, who was always willing to assist his wife in her family duties, "My dear," he said to her one evening, when their large clutch of eggs seemed almost ready to hatch, "my black feathers cannot be seen in the darkness, so *I* will guard our eggs by night, and at the same time keep them warm for you. That will leave you free to relax and enjoy yourself until daybreak each morning."

He settled down clumsily to his unaccustomed task, while his flighty wife was more than thankful to be relieved of a duty which she already found a trial. She fluffed up her feathers and, to show how pleased she was, she set off in a joyful high-stepping dance among the low termite-mounds that surrounded their nest.

The big birds had chosen the site with care, for they knew that a sitting ostrich hen, with her head down, looks from the distance like a grey mound of earth. They had decided to rear their young on the short-grassed plainlands because they could see all round them, for in those days the ostrich had a short neck like a guinea-fowl and partridge. They had learned the hard lesson that in long grass their enemies could attack them before they realized their danger.

To keep their precious eggs safe from the dreaded fires that swept across the plains, the two birds had carefully scratched away a broad band of dusty earth in the grass round the slight hollow that was their nest. On the whole they were a happy pair – although from time to time the husband had disapproved of his wife's high-spirited ways. At this particular time, she should behave more sensibly as she had her eggs to look after. He wriggled his massive thighs on the ground as he had seen his wife do, to shift the position of the eggs so that they lay more comfortably in their bed, and settled down to his long night's wait.

It was full moon. The silvery light shed strange shadows and threw up ghostly figures among the surrounding mounds of earth. His head was beginning to nod with weariness, when he became aware of his wife's hissing laugh. He was wide awake in a moment. Straining his short neck to its utmost limit, he saw her dodging in and out between the termite-mounds in a wild game of hide-and-seek with a handsome young ostrich in hot pursuit.

This would never do. He half rose from the nest – but sank down again with a sigh. He dare not leave the precious eggs, whatever the reason. What if they were to grow cold while he went to tell his flirting wife what he thought of her disgraceful behaviour?

He settled down again with a feeling of annoyance, but strained his neck further and further, to try to catch sight of her as she dodged and raced between the termite-mounds on the moonlit veld.

From time to time he *did* catch a glimpse of her, and heard her foolish giggles – and each time that he did so, he strained and stretched his neck trying to see further and yet further between the nearby termite-mounds. At last, the long, tedious night came to an end. As it did so, his wife appeared out of the grey distance to take over her duties once more.

The ostrich rose stiffly, prepared to punish

his wife for her undignified behaviour; but as he did so, he felt a strangeness in the muscles of his neck. He looked down at his feet, and was alarmed to discover how very far away from his head they were – and he realized with a shock that, as a result of all the straining that he had done during the long night, his neck had stretched, and stretched, and *stretched*. He tried to shake it back to its former length, but no matter what he did, it stayed just the same: he had stretched beyond return.

And that is why the ostrich has a long neck – a lasting memory of a flighty wife.

The Flood

Ruth Ainsworth

The shed was near the house. It was dark because it had only one small window, and that was covered with cobwebs. There were some tools in the shed, a spade and a rake and a hoe, and a pile of old sacks. There was something else as well, that not many people knew about. If you stood quite still in the shed, without moving a hand or a foot, you could hear the crackle of straw and perhaps a tiny cry.

The crackle of straw and the cry came from a box standing in a corner. In the box were a mother cat and her three newborn kittens. The cat's name was Minnie and her kittens were named One, Two, and Three. When they were big and could wash themselves and drink milk from a saucer, they would go to homes of their own. Then someone would give them proper names. But One, Two, and Three did very well to start with.

Sometimes a dog barked.

"What is that?" asked One, his little legs shaking.

"It is only Prince, the dog," purred Minnie. "He is taking care of us. He barks when he sees a stranger coming."

Sometimes a door banged.

"What is that?" mewed Two, shuddering like a jelly.

"It is only the wind blowing the door shut," purred Minnie. "Now the wind won't get into our snug bed."

Sometimes the coalman tipped the coal out with a sound like thunder.

"What is that?" cried Three, hiding her face in her mother's fur.

"It is only the coalman," purred Minnie. "His coal will make the kitchen fire blaze and burn. I will take you into the kitchen for a treat, when you are bigger, if you are very good."

A lady named Mrs Plum lived in the kitchen. She wore a white apron. Everyday she brought Minnie's meal to her, in a blue dish. When Minnie had finished her food, the dish was as clean as if it had been washed.

One night, when the kittens were fast asleep, curled like furry balls beside their mother, a storm blew up. The door and window of the shed rattled. The rain fell in floods on the roof. There were terrible claps of thunder and bright, zig-zag flashes of lightning. Even Minnie felt frightened. The river ran at the bottom of the garden, on the other side of the garden wall, and she could hear it roaring by. It sounded like a fierce growling animal.

"What is wrong? What has happened?" mewed One, Two, and Three.

"I don't know, my dears," said Minnie. "But we must go to sleep and not be frightened."

But Minnie herself was very frightened and so were the three kittens. No one could get to sleep while the storm was raging.

The kittens were so young that their eyes were not yet open. But Minnie's eyes shone like green lamps. She could see, under the door of the shed, a trickle of water. The trickle grew into a puddle. The puddle grew into a wave. The wave came nearer and nearer across the floor. Then it reached the box in the corner.

Minnie did not like water. She did not even like getting her paws wet on the wet grass. She was very, very frightened to see the water creeping under the door and spreading across the whole floor.

"If it gets any deeper," she thought to herself, "I shall take the kittens in my mouth, one at a time, and jump onto the wheelbarrow, and then up onto the shelf where the flowerpots are stacked. I don't think the water could get as high as that."

The water flowed faster and faster under the door until it was inches deep. Just when Minnie was getting ready to take a kitten in her mouth and spring onto the wheelbarrow, and then onto the shelf, a strange thing happened. The wooden box began to move about. It was floating. It was floating like a boat.

There was a thick layer of straw in the bottom of the box and an old woollen jersey. The kittens stayed dry and warm while they floated in their bed. They did not mind at all because they could not see the water as their eyes were shut.

Suddenly there was a clap of thunder and a great blast of wind. The door of the shed blew open with a bang. The water rushed in and the box swirled round and round. Then it floated out of the shed into the garden.

The river had risen so high that it swept over the garden wall. The box swished over the wall and sailed along the river which was now wide and deep like a sea. It was too dark to see exactly where they were going. Minnie cuddled her babies close to her while the rain fell in torrents. The kittens were soon fast asleep, and though Minnie was sure she would never get a wink herself, she dozed off as well.

When the morning came, they were in a watery world. There was water in front of them. Water behind. Water all round. Minnie had not known there could be so much water in one place. Strange things floated by. Branches of trees which had been torn off by the storm. Tables and chairs and pillows and cushions that had been washed out of the houses. Sacks and straw and even a dog-kennel. Minnie was pleased to see that the kennel was empty.

Nothing stopped Minnie from bringing up her kittens as well as she could, so she washed them just as carefully as if they had been on dry land. When she had finished One's face, he mewed in an excited voice:

"I can see! I can see! I can see you and Two and Three and the water and everything!"

He frisked about with joy and Minnie was afraid he might fall out of the box.

Before long, Two and Three could see as well and they spent most of the day calling out:

"What's that? What's that? What's that?" or else: "Why is the water shiny? Why is it brown?" and many other questions, some of which Minnie could not answer.

Though the kittens were well and happy, Minnie was worried. The kittens were fat as butter and could drink her warm milk whenever they wished. But there was nothing for *her* to eat, no milk – no fish – no liver. Nothing at all.

The other thing that worried her was that she could not bring her children up properly in a box floating on the water. How would they learn to lap milk from a saucer? Or walk upstairs? Or climb trees? Or catch mice? Minnie had brought up so many families of kittens that she knew exactly how the job ought to be done.

Now that the rain had stopped the floods began to go down. The river was no longer wild and roaring. Hedges and bushes could be seen that had been under the water a few hours before. When the box drifted near the bank and was caught on the branches of a willow tree, Minnie knew what she must do.

Quick as a flash, she snatched up the nearest kitten, who happened to be Two, and climbed up the tree with him. She dashed back for One and Three and the family were soon perched on the damp, slippery branch of a willow, instead of cuddled in a floating cradle filled with straw.

"This is a horrid place!" mewed One.

"I shall fall into the water and be drowned!" mewed Two.

"How are we to sleep without a bed?" mewed Three.

Minnie was not comfortable herself as she was trying to look after three young kittens as well as hold on, but she did not approve of grumbling.

"The river is going down," she said cheerfully. "Tomorrow or the next day I shall carry you home, one at a time, in my mouth. Till then, you must be good kittens and do what I tell you."

"Do you know the way home?" asked One. "We must have floated a long way in our wooden box."

Minnie was not certain that she *did* know the way, but she replied firmly:

"Of course I know the way. The river brought us here. I shall just follow the river and it will lead us home. Anyhow, all sensible cats know the way home. They never get lost."

All day and all night Minnie took care of the kittens. She fed them and washed them and sang to them, and when they slept she kept them from falling off the branch. When they were awake and wanted to play, she told them stories. She told them about the red kitchen fire that ate black coal. She told them about mice with long tails who lived in holes and were fun to chase. She told them about dear Mrs Plum and her white apron and her warm, comfortable lap.

When the *next* morning came, the river had gone right down. The ground was wet and muddy, but it was not under water. They could see the path running along the river bank.

"I shall take one of you home now," said Minnie.

"Take me!" "No, me!" "No, *me*!" mewed the three kittens. "I shall take Three first because she is the smallest," said Minnie. "Now, One and Two, be brave and sensible and hold on tightly."

"What will happen if we fall off?" asked One and Two.

"You would lose one of your nine lives," said Minnie. "Then you would have only eight left."

She took little Three in her mouth, climbed down the tree to the ground, and ran off along the river bank. She felt sure she was going the right way and that every step was bringing her nearer home. The wet mud was cold and nasty to her feet, but she did not mind. If only her three kittens were safe in front of the kitchen fire, she would never mind anything again!

Little Three squirmed and squiggled and seemed to get heavier and heavier. When at last Minnie padded slowly through the gate and up the path to the back door, she could hardly drag one foot after the other.

"Miaow! Miaow!" she cried as loudly as she could. "Miaow!"

In a second the door opened and there stood dear Mrs Plum in her white apron.

"Oh, Minnie! Minnie!" she cried, gathering Minnie and Three up in her arms, and not minding at all about the mud they left on her apron. "I thought I should never see you again!"

At first Minnie purred loudly and smiled, but she knew the job was not yet finished. She began to kick and struggle till Mrs Plum put her down on the floor. Then she ran to the back door and mewed for it to be opened.

"I know," said Mrs Plum. "I understand. You must go back for the others. Wait a moment and I will come too, I'll just make Three safe and comfortable. I kept a bed ready for all of you."

There, on the hearthrug, was another box with a soft blanket inside. Mrs Plum cuddled Three into the blanket, and Three sat and stared at the fire with round blue eyes. So *this* was the monster who ate black coal!

Mrs Plum put on her coat and hat and took a basket with a lid and opened the door. Minnie ran ahead so quickly that Mrs Plum could only just keep up. They were both tired when they got to the willow tree. Mrs Plum stood at the bottom while Minnie climbed up and found her two kittens cold and shivering, but quite safe.

"We've kept all our nine lives, Mother!" they called out.

"That's my good kittens!" said Minnie, carrying them down to the ground, where Mrs Plum stroked them and petted them and tucked them into the basket, which was lined with flannel. There was just room for Minnie as well. Then Mrs Plum carried the heavy basket home. She had to change hands when one arm ached.

When they were back in the warm kitchen, Mrs Plum gave Minnie a good meal. She had sardines and a dish of cornflakes and three saucers of milk. Then they all five settled down for a cosy afternoon by the fire. Mrs

Plum knitted in her rocking chair, and the three kittens watched the red fire eating coal and stared at the brass rim of the fender and the plates on the dresser and all the other wonderful things.

They kept looking at Mrs Plum's ball of wool

"I don't know why, but I should like to roll that ball of wool all over the floor," said One.

"So should I!" said Two and Three.

"That would be very naughty of you indeed," said Minnie. "But I wanted to do just the same when I was a kitten."

"And did you do it?" asked the three kittens.

"Yes, I'm afraid I did!" said Minnie.

She purred and smiled and dozed, as the clock ticked on the wall and the fire crackled and Mrs Plum clicked her knitting needles.

The Boy Who Turned Into a Dog

Allan Ahlberg

Eric is a boy with an extraordinary talent. He can turn into a dog! Here he has his very first taste of life in his new form – and it isn't all plain sailing. When he tries to communicate, he gets an interesting response. Whoever heard of a dog that can write!

There was once a boy who turned into a dog. The boy's name was Eric Banks; he was ten years old. The dog he turned into was a Norfolk terrier.

Eric Banks was a quiet boy, most of the time: "steady worker", "methodical", his school reports said. He was the kind of boy who didn't make a rush for the back seat of the bus, or go mad when the first snow fell. He was left-handed, right-footed and rather small for his age. He had freckles.

Eric lived with his parents and his little sister; her name was Emily, she was three. His dad was a postman; his mum had a part-time job in a shop. Eric himself had a paper round which he shared with his friend, Roy Ackerman. (Actually, he was too young to have the round. It belonged to his cousin. But she had broken her arm, and Eric's dad was a friend of the newsagent . . . so, Eric was standing in.)

Eric first turned into a dog a little at a time in his own bed. His parents were downstairs watching television. His sister was fast asleep in the next room. The time was ten past nine; the day, Wednesday; the month, June. Until then it had been a normal day for Eric. He'd done his paper round with Roy, and gone to school. He'd played with Emily before tea, and Roy after. He'd watched television, had a shower and gone to bed. Now he was *in* bed and turning into a dog.

It happened like this. Eric was lying on his

side with his eyes closed. He was almost asleep. Suddenly, he felt an itch inside the collar of his pyjama jacket. This – although he didn't know it yet – was the fur sprouting. He felt a curious tingling in his hands and feet. This was his hands and feet turning into paws. He felt his nose becoming cold and wet, his ears becoming flappy. Eric opened his eyes. He didn't panic straight away. This was his nature, partly, but also he was still half-asleep. The thought in his mind was: "I'm turning into a dog!"

That was another thing about Eric: he was a good guesser. When Emily first learned to talk, it was usually Eric who guessed what she was trying to say. He could guess the mood his teacher was in, just from the way she held her hymn-book in assembly. Now – on the evidence of a furry paw where his hand should have been – he guessed he was turning into a dog. He didn't suppose he was turning into a *werewolf*, for instance, which is what Roy Ackerman would have thought. He didn't suppose he was dreaming, either, which he was not.

The time it took Eric to turn into a dog –
his shape blurring and rippling like a
swimmer under water – was about fifteen
seconds. The time it took him to become
frantic was about five seconds after that. His
first action was to begin scrabbling in the
bed, trying to get a better look at himself. His
thoughts were in a turmoil: "I'm a dog! A
dog!" the next thing he did was try to get out
of bed. This wasn't easy for a dog in pyjamas;
besides, they were baggy on him now. Eric
leapt, and landed in a heap. He kicked his way

clear of the trousers and backed out of the jacket. He resisted the urge to growl when one of his claws got caught in the buttonhole. He sat on the floor and thought: "I'm a dog!"

It was now a quarter-past nine. The last of the evening sunlight was shining through the green curtains. Everything in the room – furniture and wallpaper, Eric's books and toys, his junior science kit, his clothes laid out on a chair beside the bed – was tinged with green light. Birds were chirruping outside the window. Next door, Mr Phipps was mowing his lawn.

Eric got to his feet – all four of them – and walked uncertainly across the room. He put his front paws on the dressing table and stared into the mirror. A furry, rather surprised-looking face stared back. "I don't believe it," he thought, and then: "I look like a Norfolk terrier." Eric knew a bit about dogs. He'd done a project on them with Roy in the second year.

Once more Eric sat on the floor. He was bewildered, to say the least. A confusion of questions jostled in his head: "How could it happen? What's the cause of it? Why me?" He went to the window, put his paws on the sill, ducked his head under the curtain and looked out. Mr Phipps was emptying the grass cuttings on to a compost heap. A wisp of blue smoke was rising from a bonfire in the next garden along. Eric left the window, and – with no clear aim in mind – nudged open the bedroom door with his head. He went on to the landing. He couldn't see much – it was gloomy – but he could smell all kinds of things. There were biscuit crumbs in the carpet. There was talcum powder. He felt the urge to sniff around. Soon he came upon a chocolate button which his sister must have dropped. She had been eating them earlier that evening. Eric studied the button. At that moment the thought in his mind was: "Being a dog might not be *all* that bad." And he ate it up.

Eric sat at the top of the stairs. He had sniffed around for other chocolate buttons without success. He'd been tempted to try his luck in Emily's room – her door was ajar as usual – but decided not to risk it. Besides, the prospects weren't good. Emily dropping her sweets was common; Emily leaving them was rare.

Now Eric cocked his head on one side. From the room below he could hear the television. In the kitchen his dad was making supper. There was a smell of coffee and cold meat. Eric felt his mouth watering, and – all at once – came to a decision: he would tell his mum and dad, that was the thing to do! After all, it wasn't as if he'd done anything wrong; wrong had been done to him.

Eric began to go downstairs. The thought occurred to him: "I wonder what's on?" and then: "Perhaps I can stay up, since I'm a dog." But going down stairs isn't easy for a dog, especially an inexperienced one. Eric found his stomach was dragging on the steps and being tickled by the carpet. What was worse, his back legs kept catching up with his front. On the last few steps he took a tumble, skidded on the hall mat and bumped into the coat-stand. After that, the sitting room door opened, the hall light went on – it was gloomy there, too – and Eric's mum appeared.

Mrs Banks looked down at him. "Charles!" she called. "We've got a dog in the house!"

A moment later Mr Banks appeared in the kitchen doorway. He saw a worried-looking Norfolk terrier on the hall mat. (Mr Banks knew about dogs. He was a postman, remember.) He crouched down and held out a hand. "Now then," he said; "How did *you* get in?"

Eric peered up at his parents. He was surprised to see how enormous they were. Their feet were huge; their heads up near the ceiling. And he was surprised that they didn't know him. Of course, there was a good reason for this, but even so . . .

Eric advanced towards his father's outstretched hand and began to speak. "I didn't get in, Dad – it's me, Eric – I've turned into a dog!"

Well, that's certainly what Eric meant to say. It's what was in his mind. However, what came out was just a string of barks and yelps. Eric tried again. It was no use. The trouble was, he had the brains of a boy, the thoughts of a boy, but the vocal chords of a dog. Mr

Banks patted his head. It occurred to him that he had seen this dog before. Its expression was . . . familiar.

Now Eric, in desperation, began prancing about. He had the idea of somehow *miming* who he was, or at least showing his parents that here was no ordinary dog. The effect was convincingly dog-like. Mrs Banks patted him also. "It's almost like he was trying to tell us something," she said. (She was a good guesser, too; unfortunately, on this occasion, not good enough.)

"Yes," said Mr Banks. "Perhaps he's trying to tell us how he got in." He took hold of Eric by the scruff of the neck and began leading him towards the door. "Come on, out you go!"

Eric didn't like the sound of this. He barked and whined. He dragged his feet.

"Sh!" said Mrs Banks. "Bad dog – you'll wake the children!"

"I *am* the children," barked Eric, "or one of them – or I was!" he struggled on a little longer. Then, sensing the hopelessness of the situation (he could hardly bite his own father), Eric gave up. He allowed himself to be led from the house and down the front path. Mrs Banks went on ahead and opened the gate. Mr Banks pushed him out on to the pavement. "Off you go," he said, and clapped his hands. "Shoo!"

Reluctantly, Eric shuffled off a few steps, then sat down. When his parents' backs were turned, he pushed his head through a gap in the fence. He watched them as they returned to the house. He heard his mum say, "I wonder how he *did* get in?" He saw the front door close.

Eric rested his muzzle on the bottom rail of the fence, and felt hard done by. A warm breeze ruffled the fur along his back. Garden smells assailed his nose. He pricked his ears to catch the distant chiming of an ice cream van. Someone across the road was playing a piano; someone was laughing. Eric stared forlornly at his own front door. He began to think of ways to get back in.

Just then a young cat came sauntering round the corner out of Clay Street. The cat saw Eric and Eric saw the cat more or less at the same time. The cat, though inexperienced, knew what was called for: it turned and ran. Eric didn't hesitate either. Here he was, a dog; abandoned on the street by his own parents *because* he was a dog. What else was he to do? It wasn't his fault. He ran after the cat.

Eric didn't catch the cat, though he tried hard enough. He chased it down Clay Street and into Apollo Road. He almost cornered it by the Ebenezer Chapel. He only lost it at the scout hut. At the scout hut, the cat left the pavement and ran up an eight-foot fence instead. (An older cat would have done something of the kind sooner.) Eric skidded to a halt. He barked and pranced about at the foot of the fence. The cat glared at him from the top, swished its tail and disappeared.

Eric stopped prancing. He barked halfheartedly at the spot where the cat had been. Now that he had time to think, he was embarrassed. He looked up and down the street to see if anyone was watching. He had his tongue out, panting – more embarrassment! Across the street, a man and a dog came out of one of the houses. Eric recognized the dog. It was a bull-mastiff he sometimes had trouble with on his paper round. His dad had trouble with it, too. The mastiff spotted him and began barking fiercely and straining on its lead. Eric couldn't understand the barks in detail, but the general meaning was clear. When he could see which way the man and dog were going, he hurried off in the opposite direction. From a safe distance he allowed himself a defiant bark for the mastiff's benefit.

Eric trotted on. He glanced back once or twice to check that he was not pursued. He began to think about his troubles. "That cat distracted me. I've got no reason to be running the streets." He was in Vernon Street now, and heading up towards the park. "Yet if I go home, I'll get put out again."

Eric slowed down and finally stopped. He looked around in a baffled way. There was an interesting smell of sausage roll in the air. He ignored it. Overhead the sky was cloudless and full of light, though it was getting late, half-past nine at least. Suddenly, Eric thought of something. He remembered the writing he'd seen scrawled on the fence which the cat had run up: DOWN WITH THE VILLA, P.L. LOVES R.V., and so on. He remembered reading it. Well – and this was the point – if he could read, he could *write*. He could go home and scratch a message in the dirt: "S.O.S. ERIC" or just "ERIC", that would do. "Mum and dad aren't stupid," he thought. "They'd never get rid of a dog who could write their own son's name in the—" he had another idea – "Emily's sandpit, that was the place!"

Eric at once became impatient to try out his idea. Luckily, on Vernon Street there were grass verges between the front gardens and the pavement. He soon found a bare patch suitable for his purpose. He looked around. Two girls with tennis rackets were coming down the street. He waited for them to pass. A woman with a pram went by on the opposite side. A car and a couple of cyclists came and went. Then it was clear.

Eric sat up straight and extended his left paw. He brushed a sweet-paper and a bit of twig from his chosen spot. He began to write "E . . . R . . .," he scratched his letters in the dusty earth. It reminded him of the sand-tray at Mrs Parry's play school years ago. "It's going to work," he thought. "E . . . R . . . I . . . C . . . I can do it!"

When he'd finished, Eric put his head on one side and stared at the result. "Needs to be neater, though – that R's no good." He scrubbed out what he had written and began again. He became for a time engrossed in the quality of his writing. (If Mrs Jessop – she

was his teacher – could've seen him then! Eric was not always so particular.)

All of a sudden he was aware of being watched. He heard a voice say, "Here, Jack – come and look at this dog!" From the nearby garden a large woman was peering at him over a hedge. She had her hair in rollers and was holding a watering can. "He's writing – in the dirt!"

From the direction of the house a man's voice said, "Geroff!"

"Yes he is – he's stopped now – he's scrubbing it out!"

"Geroff!" said the man.

Eric considered the situation and decided to leave. He set off up the street. "E . . . R . . . I . . . C," he heard the woman say. "'Eric', that's what he wrote."

"Geroff!" the man said. There was a burst of laughter. "That's no name for a dog!"

The Lioness and the Mouse

Retold by Robin Lister

Simba was tired. Of course she was. So would you be if you got up before dawn to hunt breakfast. Especially if breakfast turned out to be very fast on its feet and ran away from you. Simba had chased the zebra for mile after mile across the dusty plain before making the kill. Then she had dragged it all the way back home to her waiting cubs. It was a dog's life being a lioness.

As usual, each cub wanted the lion's share:

"I want leg, I want leg," shouted the first cub.

"You always have it, it's my turn," shrieked the second.

"He's got more than me," yelped the third.

"More, more, more," screamed the fourth.

"S'not fair, s'not fair, s'not fair!" squawked the fifth (she was quite right; s'never fair).

"Oh, shut up," roared Simba. "You're behaving like a lot of spoilt children. Just remember that you're lions. It's all good meat and there's plenty for everybody. So not another murmur."

After that the cubs were as quiet as mice. Which was very sensible because their mother was a lioness, after all, and she had huge paws and razor-sharp claws.

"Right, you lot," growled Simba, as soon as they had finished, "Mummy's going to have a rest and she doesn't want to be disturbed. So run along and play among yourselves. And remember, no squabbling."

She yawned and her cubs could see right inside her cavernous mouth. It was lined with two rows of enormous pointed teeth. You don't argue with teeth like that, thought the little cubs, and off they ran to play.

Simba padded down to the water-hole for a long, refreshing drink. Then she settled in the long grass in the shade of a great tree. Peace and quiet at last. Lions just don't realize how much we lionesses have to do, she thought, as she began to doze. It's all very well for lions; they just lie around all day – and all night too, as often as not. Her lion was like that. Just because of his great mane and beard, he thought he was too good to help with the cubs. But she was much too exhausted to bother about all this for long and soon she fell into a deep sleep.

Mouse was tired too. He had spent the night running away from Owl, who had already eaten his mother, father, sister, brother, and his great-aunt Squeak. It's a dog's life being a mouse, thought Mouse, as he crept through the long grass into the shade of the great tree. The soft, warm, golden, furry heap he burrowed into was just what he had been looking for.

"The perfect place to lie on," murmured Mouse out loud, as he made himself comfortable. He was just beginning to drift off into sleep when something rough, sharp and very powerful seized him by the throat.

Simba was dreaming of a magical world where lions did all the work and the lionesses lay about sleeping and playing games. It was a delightful dream and she was not at all pleased to be woken up. When she saw what was in her paw she could hardly believe her eyes. A mouse! A tiny little mouse on a great lioness. Mouse was terrified.

"Oh dear," squeaked Mouse, "I'm-m-m-m-m-most terribly sorry."

"Sorry!" roared Simba. "Sorry, you snivelling little rodent! I'll make you sorry all right."

She raised her other paw. It would soon be all over for Mouse.

"No, mighty Simba, I beg you, don't do it. It was all a dreadful mousetake."

"Mousetake! Mousetake! Thought I was dead did you? Well listen to me, young man. Even if I were dead and stuffed full of straw in a natural history museum you should show respect – and I mean respect – to me, a great lioness. You've no excuse."

"Oh Simba, Simba," pleaded Mouse, who was ready to try anything, "you're much too important to bother with a wretched little thing like me. In any case I'm sure I'll taste disgusting."

Simba screwed up her great cat's face.

"Me eat you? Eat a mouse? Ugh! Lionesses don't eat mice, young man. They eat antelope, zebra, and cattle. Besides, I'm not in the least bit hungry. Eat a mouse, ha! What a load of mousetrap, I mean claptrap."

"Oh dear, oh dear, oh dear," said Mouse, more desperate than ever. "Please, please please don't kill me. Since my life is worth nothing, my death is worth even less. And if I live, who knows, I may be able to help you one day."

Simba roared again, only this time with laughter.

"Ha, ha, ha, ho, ho, ho! You help me. That's rich. A mouse help a lioness. Now I've heard everything."

She looked at the tiny creature clamped in her paw. There was a twinkle in her smouldering brown eyes.

"Go on then, scarper, before anyone sees us. It would ruin my reputation if it got around that I'd gone soft on mice."

Mouse scurried off into the undergrowth, grateful for his escape but more exhausted than ever. There's just no future in being a mouse, he thought, wishing he were a hundred times the size, like Simba, for instance.

But big as she was, Simba was in trouble. As Mouse scurried away, a crack of a gunshot echoed behind him. Simba leaped up in pain and then fell to the ground. She struggled to get up again but she felt too weak. She had been shot with a tranquillizer. As she lay there, unable to move, a group of men came out of the cover of the trees and threw a net over her. She was trapped. Moments later she fainted. When Simba woke she felt terrible. Her head ached and the net bit into her skin. She couldn't move, and when she tried to roar for help her voice was pitifully weak. Her whole body was sore. They had dragged her a long way.

"It's all over for me," she moaned. "They'll take me somewhere cold and wet and stick me in a smelly little cage. People will bring their children to point at me through the bars. And I'll never see my little cubs again."

Tears sprang into Simba's eyes and rolled down her cheeks.

Mouse was out of breath: "Phew!" he panted. "At last."

He was only a little mouse and already very tired. It had been hard work keeping up with the men. After a few minutes he got his breath back.

"Right," he squeaked briskly. "There's no time to waste. You just lie there, Simba, and watch this."

He began to gnaw at the net. It was made of special tough rope but Mouse had specially sharp little teeth. He had soon bitten through it in several places, and Simba managed to get her paws through the holes and do the rest. She was very grateful.

"Mouse," she purred, when they were miles away and safe. "I'm very sorry I laughed at you. It just goes to show that size isn't everything. I don't know how to thank you!"

"Don't mention it, mighty Simba, don't mention it. And now, if you don't mind, I'll go to sleep again."

Mouse burrowed deeper into the soft, warm, golden, furry heap without a care in the world. Perhaps it wasn't so bad being a mouse after all.

Delilah the Spider

Colin Thompson

Delilah the spider sat very still in the corner of the window and waited. There was a fat bluebottle buzzing round the empty room and she knew if she waited long enough it would get caught in her web. A window is the best place for a spider's web because flies spend half their lives crashing into the glass. If they are outside they keep trying to get in, and if they are inside they keep trying to get out.

"Insects are very stupid," thought Delilah, "But very tasty."

A couple of mosquitoes that she was saving for lunch wriggled in their silk prison and a blue-tit hung on the window trying to peck them through the glass.

"Birds are very stupid too," thought Delilah, "but I wouldn't want to eat one."

It was a beautiful clear autumn morning and when the sun had warmed the air Delilah had gone outside and laid three hundred and twenty eggs. They were wrapped in a soft yellow cocoon under the window sill, sheltered from the wind and rain. Next summer they would hatch and her babies would eat their way down the honeysuckle into the garden. Some of them would wriggle through the gap into the house and Delilah would probably eat them.

"Babies are very stupid," she thought, "but very tender."

When she had finished laying her eggs she had come back into the house and eaten her husband Nigel.

"Husbands are very stupid," she thought, "and very slow."

The bluebottle flew round and round the bare light bulb and then dived straight into Delilah's web. It hung there caught by its leg and buzzed furiously. The louder it buzzed and wriggled the more it got caught and the more it got caught the louder it buzzed.

"Look, stupid fly, do you think you could keep the noise down?" snapped Delilah. "I've got a terrible headache."

She raced across the silken ladders and rolled the fly up into a parcel, but even when she had wrapped it tight it kept buzzing, so she ate it.

"The mosquitoes will keep till tomorrow," she thought.

There were other spiders in the room, but none on Delilah's window. She had chased them away into the dark corners where all they ever caught were dust mites and midges.

"Spiders are stupid," said Delilah.

"You think everyone's stupid, don't you?" said a little brown spider called Norma from behind the skirting board.

"That's the only intelligent thing you've ever said," replied Delilah.

"I think you're horrible," said the little brown spider.

"Two intelligent remarks in one day," sneered Delilah. "If you're not careful your pathetic little brain will explode."

Norma said nothing, not because her brain had exploded, but because she was busy thinking of a way to get rid of Delilah.

It was bad enough now the house was empty, without Delilah making everyone's life a misery. There was no one to open the windows so hardly any flies came in. Without humans there were no smells of sticky jam and pies to attract them. What few bits of food the old lady had left had been eaten by the rats. It was all right for the spiders out in the garden, but as everyone knows there are thousands of spiders to every square yard and they certainly wouldn't make room for all the house spiders.

"It's not as if she's anything special like a tarantula," said Norma. "She's just a common house spider like the rest of us."

"She's got the best place in the room and won't let any of us near it," said Norma's neighbour Sybil.

"You don't have to tell me," agreed Norma. "Look what happened when Edwina tried to make a web at the other end of the window."

"Well yes, I know," said Sybil. "She got eaten. I mean, Delilah even ate her own husband."

"Something will have to be done," said Norma with a firm stamp of several feet.

Something had to be done. That was obvious. The rest of the spiders, from the coal black shadows of the cellar to the draughty slates on the roof, all managed to live together with no trouble. Sometimes if a strange spider came too close to another's web it got eaten but that was perfectly natural and no one got upset about it. The spider doing the eating had a friendly word with its dinner and everyone knew where they were.

Delilah on the other hand had been nothing but trouble since the day she'd hatched. Within a week she had eaten all her brothers and sisters and her mother. She was as rude and vicious as she could be to everyone. If she couldn't eat them she swore at them. Something had to be done.

"Maybe we could set fire to her web while she's asleep," suggested Sybil.

"Only humans can do that," said Norma.

"Maybe we could get a wasp to sting her," said Sybil.

"Do you want to go and ask one?" asked Norma. Sybil didn't. She knew that wasps were one of the spiders' greatest enemies.

"Well, we've got to do something," she said.

"It's all right," said Norma. "I have a plan."

Norma's plan was the sort of plan that you make up as you go along. She knew what she wanted to do but she wasn't quite sure how to do it.

Every night under cover of darkness, all the spiders from the upstairs rooms built a huge web across the other side of the room from Delilah. Delilah could see it growing each day but she was far too important to take any interest in it. She was more concerned with her dinner. Since she had eaten the two mosquitoes three days before she hadn't caught a single thing and was beginning to feel hungry. She slid down to the floor and stole a flea from Sybil's web and when Sybil protested she ate her.

"Not only are spiders stupid," she said, "they taste rotten." The other spiders said

nothing. Across the room they hid under their gigantic web and waited.

In the next room there was a broken window that had been covered up with cardboard. The spiders chewed at the sticky tape until the cardboard fell away. A blast of cold air blew into the room and ten minutes later two huge flies came through the hole and flew straight into the trap the spiders had woven behind it. That night the spiders carried the two flies up into the giant web and wrapped them up just enough to stop them escaping but not to stop them buzzing loudly.

Across the room Delilah woke up and heard the imprisoned flies. She could see them right in the middle of the web the stupid spiders had made and her mouth started watering. She scuttled round the wall and out along the silk rope towards the delicious feast. She was so hungry she felt quite dizzy and didn't notice the other spiders hiding at the corners of the web with their teeth in the threads. She reached the flies and as she did so the whole web went crashing to the ground.

"Stupid spiders," thought Delilah as she ate the flies. "Can't even build a web properly."

"Delilah, Delilah," called a voice softly from above.

"Drop dead," snarled Delilah.

"Are you enjoying your last meal?" called the voice.

"Last meal?" laughed Delilah. "I'll eat you next, idiot."

"I don't think so," said the voice.

Delilah looked round. Through the tangle

of the web she could see the white walls of the room. There was something strange about them, though. They had become all shiny like glass. Suddenly, she realized where she was but by then it was too late. Round and round she ran but it was no use.

"Bye-bye, Delilah," called the voice. It was Norma, sitting on the bath tap, looking down into Delilah's prison.

Heaven

David Henry Wilson

The gerbils were dead. Daddy had bought them on the twins' first birthday, and so Jeremy James had christened them Wiffer and Jeffer. He'd loved to hold them, and to watch them chasing round their cage, burrowing in the sawdust, or treadling their wheel. But last night they had both been lying quietly, and this morning they were lying dead.

"What made them die?" asked Jeremy James through his tears.

"Difficult to say without a post-mortem," answered Daddy.

"Will the postman bring one?" asked Jeremy James.

"A post-mortem's an examination," said

Daddy, "to find the cause of death."

Jeremy James didn't want to examine Wiffer and Jeffer. He didn't even want to look at them lying there so still and stiff in the corner of their cage.

There had been a death in the family before. Great-Great-Aunt Maud had died at the age of ninety-two, and Jeremy James had gone to her funeral. She had been put in a beautiful shiny box, which Jeremy James would have liked to keep his toys and sweets in. Only the grown-ups had wasted it by putting it in the ground and covering it up with earth.

"We'll just bury them, shall we?" said Daddy. "Somewhere nice in the garden."

"Will we put them in a box?" asked Jeremy James. "Like Great-Great-Aunt-Maud?"

"Yes," said Daddy. "Maybe you can go and find one, while I get things ready."

Jeremy James remembered something else about Great-Great-Aunt Maud.

"Can we have a party afterwards as well?" he asked.

"I expect Mummy will let us have a few

sandwiches and cakes," said Daddy.

It so happened that Mummy had already planned to make sandwiches and cakes, because the Reverend Cole was coming round to discuss the church fête.

"Maybe if you ask him nicely," said Mummy, "the Reverend Cole might give the gerbils a proper burial."

Jeremy James thought that was a good idea, and so off he went to look for a box, while Mummy made the sandwiches and cakes, and Daddy went out into the garden to dig a grave.

The box that Jeremy James chose was bright and cheerful. Great-Great-Aunt Maud had been buried in one that was heavy and shiny and dark, but she'd been very old, and so maybe she hadn't liked cheerful boxes. The gerbils would have one that was covered in different-coloured blobs, each of which was a pleasure to look at whether you were alive or dead. It was an empty liquorice allsort box.

The Reverend Cole was very old, too, though not as old or as dead as Great-Great-Aunt Maud. He walked with a hobble, and talked with a wobble, and he had accidentally dropped Christopher in the font during the twins' christening. Jeremy James remembered that day very well, because he had accidentally been the cause of the Reverend Cole accidentally dropping Christopher.

"Never heard of dead marbles," said the Reverend Cole.

"Not marbles," said Jeremy James. "Gerbils."

"Ah!" said the Reverend Cole. "Where are they, then?"

"Here," said Jeremy James, holding out the liquorice allsort box.

"Thank you," said the Reverend Cole. "My favourite sweets."

He took the box, opened the lid, and found himself looking at Wiffer and Jeffer.

"Aaaugh!" he cried, and promptly dropped the box on the floor. Wiffer and Jeffer fell out on to the carpet, while the Reverend Cole did a sort of hobble-jump backwards, bumped straight into the coffee table, and knocked off the teapot that Mummy had just put there.

"Aaaugh!" cried the Reverend Cole again,

as hot tea splashed over his leg and foot. Then he hobble-hopped to an armchair, and hobble-slumped into it.

"Oh dear!" said Mummy. "I'm ever so sorry."

She fetched a couple of cloths, and while she wiped the Reverend Cole's shoe and trouser leg, Daddy mopped up the tea from the carpet. Meanwhile, Wiffer and Jeffer lay next to the liquorice allsort box, and Jeremy James stood looking at them, with tears dropping out of his eyes.

Eventually, Daddy put them back in their box, Mummy made some more tea, and the Reverend Cole patted Jeremy James on the head.

"No harm done," he said. "Just a drop o' spilt tea. No need to cry."

Jeremy James hadn't been crying because of the spilt tea, but with Wiffer and Jeffer safely back in their box, he stopped crying, and the Reverend Cole congratulated himself on his handling of the situation.

Daddy had dug a little grave under the apple tree, and very solemnly everyone trooped out into the garden. Mummy was holding Christopher, Daddy was holding Jennifer, Jeremy James was holding the box, and the Reverend Cole held forth:

"O Death," he said, "where is thy sting? O grave, where is thy victory? Oh Jeremy James, where is thy box?"

Jeremy James stepped forward with the box.

"Just put it in the . . . um . . . grave, will you?"

Jeremy James put the box in the grave.

"Forasmuch as the souls of these . . . um . . . gerbils here departed are in the care of Almighty God," said the Reverend Cole, "we therefore commit their bodies to the ground; earth to earth, ashes to ashes, dust to dust; in sure and certain . . . um . . . possible hope of eternal life, through our Lord Jesus Christ."

Beside the grave was a little pile of earth, which Daddy now pushed over the box until it was completely covered. Then the family went back into the house, and Mummy produced the sandwiches and cakes that were such an important part of any funeral.

"Will the gerbils be in Heaven now?" Jeremy James asked the Reverend Cole, through a mouthful of fruit cake.

"Ah!" said the Reverend Cole, through a mouthful of salmon sandwich. "That's a very good question."

Since he showed no sign of answering it, Jeremy James asked him again.

"Many people do believe that animals have souls," he said, "and if they do, then I'm sure the gerbils will be in Heaven."

"What's a soul?" asked Jeremy James.

"It's the part of you that never dies," said the Reverend Cole. "It's your soul that goes to Heaven."

"Have I got one?" asked Jeremy James.

"Certainly," said the Reverend Cole.

"Where is it?" asked Jeremy James.

"Somewhere inside you," said the Reverend Cole.

Jeremy James would have liked to ask a lot more questions about his soul, but Mummy and the Reverend Cole had to talk about the fête, and so Jeremy James turned his thoughts to fruit cake instead.

That night, Jeremy James couldn't get to sleep. He was thinking about the gerbils and Heaven and his soul. He had asked Mummy and Daddy where his soul was, but their answer had been just as vague as the Reverend Cole's: "Hmmph" (Mummy) and "Worple worple" (Daddy).

He'd also asked them where Heaven was. Mummy thought it might be somewhere beyond the stars, and Daddy thought it was the football ground after a home win.

The problem for Jeremy James was that if the Reverend Cole was right, and the soul was inside you, it would have to get out and find its way to Heaven. How could it do that if it didn't know – or if you didn't know – where Heaven was? Daddy, for instance, couldn't even find his way round London, so how would *he* get to Heaven?

"I expect someone comes to guide you," Mummy had said.

And that was keeping Jeremy James awake. Nobody had come to guide the gerbils. They'd simply been lying in their cage, then they'd been put in the liquorice allsort box, and buried under the apple tree. He would have *seen* if anyone had come to guide them.

Great-Great-Aunt Maud had been buried on a Saturday. Jeremy James remembered that very well, because Daddy had wanted to go to a football match, and on their way home, they'd had to drive through the crowd. But she hadn't died on the Saturday. She'd died before. So why hadn't she been buried on the day she died?

The answer was obvious. You had to wait till the guide had come before you put the body in the box and buried it. But the gerbils *had* been buried on the day they'd died. And now their souls would be trying to get out of the box and out of the ground before the guide came, because otherwise he'd never find them, would go away, and they would never get to Heaven.

Jeremy James reached for his torch, climbed out of bed, put on his slippers, and opened the bedroom door. The whole house was dark and silent. Everyone was asleep.

Jeremy James crept downstairs, unbolted

the kitchen door, and made his way across the lawn to the apple tree.

The following morning, when she looked out of the kitchen window, Mummy was surprised to see a brightly-coloured box lying under the apple tree. She knew at once what it was, and when she went out to take a closer look she found the lid open, and the two gerbils inside, just as dead as ever. She hastily closed the lid, put the box back in its hole, and covered it up.

"I suppose it must have been a dog," she said to Daddy when he came downstairs.

"I shouldn't think a dog would have left them lying there," said Daddy.

But neither of them could think of a better explanation, and they agreed not to tell Jeremy James, because they didn't want to upset him.

Jeremy James didn't wake up till quite late that morning, but as soon as he went downstairs, he wanted to go and look at the gerbils' grave.

"A good thing you spotted it," said Daddy to Mummy, when Jeremy James had gone.

"Imagine what he'd have felt if he'd seen them lying there."

When Jeremy James returned, there was a big smile on his face.

"You're looking very pleased with yourself," said Daddy.

And Jeremy James *was* pleased with himself. He knew that the guide had come in the night and taken the gerbils (and the liquorice allsort box) to Heaven. But he decided not to tell Mummy and Daddy. They didn't know enough about souls or about Heaven to really understand.

Rabbits Go Riding

Anita Hewett

Up sprang Kangaroo, with long, strong leaps. And *down* came Kangaroo, thumping on the ground.

"Carry my leaves in your pocket," called Koala, and he threw them into Kangaroo's pouch.

"They prickle," said Kangaroo, but over the spinifex grass she leapt.

"Carry my ants," called little Echidna, and he threw them into Kangaroo's pouch.

"They tickle," said Kangaroo, but over the yellow wattles she leapt.

"Carry my frog in your pocket," called Snake.

"It's cold and jumpy," said Kangaroo, but on she went between the gum trees.

"Carry my pineapple," Possum called.

"It's hard and lumpy," said Kangaroo, but on she went, over scrubland and plain.

Kangaroo jumped with short, tired hops, with the leaves that prickled, the ants that tickled, the jumpy frog, and the lumpy pineapple. Her pouch looked just like a shopping basket.

"Now I am home at last," she sighed, and she lay in the dust bath beneath her tree.

"Thank you," the lazy creatures said. "You can carry our things again tomorrow."

"Oh, I'm so tired," sighed Kangaroo. "But they *will* keep throwing their things in my pouch."

Then she lay in the shade and tried to sleep.

A little later she opened her eyes. Two fat rabbits sat side by side. Kangaroo saw that their fur was ruffled. Their paws were sore, and their tails were dusty.

"Please, Mrs Kangaroo," they said. "Which is the way to the farmer's grassland?"

Kangaroo looked towards the hills, which were blue, and misty, and far away.

"Between the gum trees and over the hills,

at the end of a long black road," she said.

The rabbits sat down on their dusty white tails, and stared at each other with tears in their eyes.

"Then we'll never get home tonight," they said. "We're tired, and lost, and a little bit frightened. We want to go home. We want it so much."

Kangaroo looked at the sad little rabbits. Then she stretched her aching legs, and said: "Jump in my pocket. I'll carry you home."

The fat grey rabbits jumped in her pouch.

"We are ready to start, when you are," they said.

Kangaroo jumped between the gum trees. The rabbits felt soft and warm in her pouch. They wriggled and giggled and squealed with delight.

"Thump, we are down, we are down," they said. "Up, we are up. We are down. We are up."

"Carry my leaves in your pocket," called Koala, and he threw them into Kangaroo's pouch.

"Rubbish," giggled the fat grey rabbits, and they scooped up the leaves in their strong little paws, and threw them back at Koala.

Kangaroo reached the foot of the hills.

"Carry my ants," called little Echidna, and he threw them into Kangaroo's pouch.

"Tickly things!" the rabbits squealed. "They'll get in our fur." And they threw them away.

Kangaroo leapt to the top of the hills.

"Carry my frog in your pocket," called Snake, and he threw it into Kangaroo's pouch.

"Full up! No room!" called the fat grey

rabbits, and they tossed the jumping frog in a salt bush.

Kangaroo reached the long black road.

"Carry my pineapple," Possum called, and he threw it into Kangaroo's pouch.

"No thanks! We're not hungry," the rabbits shouted, and the pineapple bounced as it fell on the road.

"Thump, we are down. We are up," squeaked the rabbits. "Thump, we are up. We are down. We are home."

Kangaroo lay in the long cool grass. The rabbits climbed out of her pouch and said, "We've had such a wonderful ride in your pocket. Thank you for bringing us home so quickly."

Kangaroo smiled.

"It was easy," she said. "Those lazy creatures were *very* surprised. They won't make me carry their things again."

She was right, and never, never again did her pouch look just like a shopping basket. Nor was it empty every day as she leapt over spinifex grass and hill, because over its edge peeped two furry faces.

"Here we go riding again," squeaked the rabbits.

"Thump, we are down. We are up. We are down. Thump! We are riding in Kangaroo's pocket."

The Happiest Woodlouse

Dick King-Smith

Walter was a wimp. He was scared of his own shadow – always had been since he was tiny.

No matter that he was now a really big woodlouse, with fourteen strong legs and a fine coat of armour, Walter was still afraid of everything and anything. Spiders, black beetles, centipedes, earwigs – whatever kind of creature he met frightened the life out of him, so that he rolled himself into a ball and wouldn't unroll again for ages.

Even with other woodlice he was just the same. Every time he met one, he rolled up and stayed rolled up until the patter of fourteen feet had died away in the distance.

You can easily understand why Walter had no friends.

I would like to make a friend, he said to himself. I would like to be able to have a good chat with someone, crack a joke or two perhaps. It must be nice to have a pal. If only I wasn't so nervous.

At that moment he heard someone approaching the large flat stone under which he was sheltering, and hastily he curled himself into a ball. The footsteps came nearer, and suddenly, to his horror, Walter felt himself being nudged. It was the sort of hefty nudge, Walter thought, that some fierce creature might give a wretched woodlouse before picking it up and swallowing it whole.

But then he heard a voice. It was a jolly voice which did not sound fierce but friendly.

"Wakey! Wakey!" said the voice. "What's a chap like you doing all curled up on a nice sunny day like this, eh?"

Could this be the friend I've been waiting for, thought Walter?

"What are you?" he said, in somewhat muffled tones, for it is hard to speak when you are curled up in a ball.

"I'm a woodlouse of course, like you," said the voice. "Come on, unroll, why don't you? Anyone would think you were afraid of something."

If you only knew, said Walter to himself, I'm afraid of everything, but all the same he unrolled, to find himself face to face with a woodlouse of about his own size, but of a slightly different colour. Walter was slaty-grey. This stranger was paler, sort of brownish in fact, and freckled all over.

Walter waved his antennae.

"Hello," he said. "I'm Walter."

"Hi," said the stranger, waving back.

He looks a decent sort of chap, thought Walter. Well, it's now or never, so he took a deep breath and said, "Will you be my friend?"

"My!" said the freckly stranger. "You're a fast worker!"

"How do you mean?" said Walter.

"You don't waste time, do you? No remarks about the weather, no polite chit-chat, just 'Will you be my friend?' Fair takes a girl's breath away!"

A girl, thought Walter! I just wanted a pal to have a chat with and crack a joke, but a girlfriend! Oh no, I'm frightened of girls. He was just about to curl up again when the stranger said, "OK."

Walter hesitated.

"OK what?" he said.

"OK, I'll be your friend, Walter. I've seen worse-looking woodlice than you. By the way, my name's Marilyn."

"Oh," said Walter.

He wiggled several pairs of legs nervously.

"I'm pleased to meet you," he said.

"You're a funny boy," said Marilyn with a light laugh, and she moved forward until her antennae brushed gently against his.

At this touch something like an electric shock ran through every plate of Walter's armour and he found himself suddenly very short of breath.

"Come on," said Marilyn. "Let's go for a stroll."

Ordinarily Walter never came out from beneath his large flat stone till nightfall. Spiders and black beetles and centipedes and earwigs were frightening enough, but in daylight, out in the open, there was far worse danger. Birds! Birds with sharp eyes and sharper beaks that snapped up spiders and black beetles and centipedes and earwigs – and woodlice!

"Can't we wait till after dark, Marilyn?" he said.

Marilyn giggled.

"Oh, you are a one!" she said, and out she went and off along the garden path.

Despite himself, Walter followed. He was frightened, terrified indeed, but he hurried after Marilyn as fast as his seven pairs of legs could carry him. How beautiful she was, he now could see. Her long antennae, the slender legs, each delicate joint of her freckled carapace – all were perfection. Here, in the wide open spaces of the garden, death might threaten, but without Marilyn, thought Walter, life would not be worth living.

"Wait for me!" he called, but even as he spoke he saw to his horror that in the middle of the path ahead there squatted a huge slimy monster.

"Marilyn!" he cried. "Watch out!" and hastily he rolled himself into a ball. Miserably he waited, tightly curled. Cruel Fate, thought Walter. I meet the love of my life and within minutes she walks down a monster's throat. If only I were brave, I might have tackled the brute. But I'm not, alas, I'm not.

Then a voice said, "Are you coming, Walter, or aren't you!"

"What were you playing at?" said Marilyn

when, sheepishly, he caught up with her. Of the monster there was no sign but a trail of slime across the flagstones.

Walter gulped.

"I thought I saw a monster," he said.

"Monster?" said Marilyn. "That was only an old slug. Mind where you're putting your feet, the path's all sticky."

They walked on, off the path and on to a rose-bed under whose bushes was a scattering of dead leaves. On these they began to browse, side by side.

"Walter," said Marilyn.

"Yes, Marilyn?"

"You've got a yellow streak, haven't you?"

Walter did not answer.

"Not to mince words," said Marilyn, "you're a chicken-hearted scaredy-cat and a cowardy-custard, aren't you?"

"Yes," said Walter.

"Well, at least you've been honest with me," said Marilyn, "so I'll do the same for you. Let's just forget the friendship bit. You're a nice boy, but if there's one thing I can't stand, it's a wimp. No hard feelings, eh?"

"But, Marilyn." said Walter.

"Yes?"

"I . . . I love you."

For a moment Marilyn gazed thoughtfully at Walter. Such a good-looking fellow, but no backbone. Shame, really.

"Sorry, Walter," she said. "See you around, maybe," and she turned to go.

As she did so, Walter saw the thrush come hopping through the rose-bed, straight towards her.

Even as he tensed his muscles to roll himself into a ball, something snapped in his brain, and instead he rushed forward on his fourteen powerful legs.

"Roll up, quick!" he shouted at Marilyn, shoving her out of his way, and then, as instinctively she obeyed, Walter made directly for the huge bird.

"Take me!" he cried. "Take me, you brute, but spare my Marilyn!"

The thrush put its head on one side, the better to focus upon this foolhardy woodlouse, when it saw from the corner of its other eye a fat worm. Leaving Walter for afters, it picked up the worm and swallowed it.

As it was doing so, a large tabby cat came strolling down the garden path, waving its tail, and the thrush flew hastily away.

"All clear!" cried Walter, and Marilyn unrolled.

"You saved my life!" she breathed.

"Well, I don't know about that," said Walter in an embarrassed voice.

"Well, you jolly well tried to," said Marilyn. "You were ready to sacrifice yourself to protect me, weren't you?"

"Yes," said Walter.

Marilyn stared at her gallant knight in armour.

To think, she said to herself, that I called him a cowardy-custard. Her heart swelled within her bosom, and she went weak at the knees, all fourteen of them.

"Oh Walter," she said softly, "I am yours, all yours."

"Oh Marilyn," said Walter. "You have made me the happiest woodlouse in the world!"

Tod and the Desperate Search

Philippa Pearce

The next-door neighbour, old Mr Parkin, was going away for a week's holiday. But what was going to happen to his cat, Ginger, while he was away?

"Can't Mr Parkin take Ginger on holiday with him?" asked Tod. "Wouldn't Ginger like a holiday?"

"Cats like staying at home," said Tod's mother. "Your dad and I have offered to feed Ginger while Mr Parkin's away; and Mr Parkin has said, Yes please. He's given me his back-door key, so that we can go into the house and get the cat-food every day. Ginger has half a tin of cat-food every morning and another half tin every evening."

"My, that's a lot for a cat!" said Tod's father.

"Ginger's a big cat," said Tod's mother.

Tod said, "Can I come with you when you go to feed Ginger?"

"Of course," said his mother; and his father said, "You could be a great help, Tod."

So it was settled.

Ginger was a big cat, yellowy-brown all over except for one white front leg. He was rather a silent cat. He never miaowed; but he purred when he was tickled behind his ear. He liked to be out of doors most of the time.

On the first morning after old Mr Parkin had gone on holiday, Tod was at home with his father. They took Mr Parkin's key and went round to the back of his house. There was Ginger at the back door, his tail waving high in the air, ready for his breakfast. They unlocked the door and went into Mr Parkin's kitchen, Ginger slipping in ahead of them. Mr Parkin had left his kitchen very neat and clean; and the door between the kitchen and the rest of the house was shut. This was so that Ginger could not go wandering off through the other rooms.

Tod's father opened a tin of cat-food, while Tod washed the cat-dish that Ginger had eaten his supper from the evening before. Ginger had two cat-dishes to eat from, one being used, one being washed. So he always had a clean dish for his food.

Tod's father put down the clean dish with half a tin of cat-food in it. Ginger began eating very fast.

While Ginger ate, Tod's father put the half-used tin into the fridge; and Tod fetched Ginger's water bowl that always stood just outside the back door. He emptied the old water away and refilled the bowl with clean, fresh water from the tap and put the bowl outside again.

By now Ginger had finished his breakfast and he walked out into the garden again, very pleased with himself. He settled on the lawn in a patch of sunshine and began cleaning his fur.

"But where will he sleep tonight?" asked Tod.

"If it's cold," said Tod's father, "he can get through the cat door into the boiler house. It's always warm in there, and Mr Parkin has put a basket there with an old blanket in it. But if the night's not cold, then Ginger will probably sleep out in the garden under a bush."

Tod's father locked Mr Parkin's back door again. They said goodbye to Ginger and went back to their own house.

That evening Tod didn't go with his mother – it was her turn – to give Ginger his supper, because he was being bathed and put to bed by his father. But every morning Tod went with his mother or his father to give Ginger his breakfast, wash a cat-dish, and renew the water in the drinking bowl.

And every morning there was Ginger at Mr Parkin's back door, tail in the air, eager for his breakfast.

Then one morning, almost at the end of Mr Parkin's week away from home, Tod went as usual with his father, and Ginger was not waiting at Mr Parkin's back door.

"Bother," said Tod's father. "That cat's late for his breakfast." And he began to call him: "Ginger! Ginger!"

No Ginger came.

"You call him, Tod," said his father.

So Tod called him: "Ginger! Ginger!" and then "Ginger-ninger!" and then "Ginger-winger!"

They both called and called, but no cat came. In the end they decided to leave the dish of cat-food just outside the back door, with fresh water in the drinking bowl. Perhaps Ginger would come later.

At midday Tod and his father went round to Mr Parkin's back door again. There was the dish of cat-food still. It looked as if birds might have pecked at it; but most of the food remained. Ginger would have eaten the whole lot and left the dish clean. So Ginger had not been.

When Tod's mother came home, they told her about Ginger's having gone missing. "What a worry!" she said. "Mr Parkin's back the day after tomorrow. I don't know what he'll say if Ginger's not there to greet him."

"Perhaps the cat's got shut in somewhere," said Tod's father.

"Perhaps in Mr Parkin's house," said Tod.

"No," said his mother. "You remember the door from the kitchen into the rest of the house has always been kept shut. And Mr Parkin told me himself that he shut and locked every window in the house, upstairs and down, before he left."

"There's still his garden shed and his greenhouse and that boiler house," said Tod's father. "We must search everywhere."

So all three of them went to look in Mr Parkin's garden shed and his greenhouse and the boiler house. They even came back and looked in their own garden shed.

No Ginger anywhere.

They began to feel desperate.

Tod had never before helped to give Ginger his supper; but today, after this bath, he put on his pyjamas and his dressing gown and his bedroom slippers and went round with his mother and his father to see if Ginger had turned up for his supper.

He hadn't.

Tod's mother said, "I hope that he hasn't strayed on to the main road and been run over by a car."

"I think Ginger's probably too sensible for that," said Tod's father.

Tod said, "I don't want Ginger to be dead."

His parents comforted him. They mustn't give up hope yet, they said. Who knows? Ginger might still turn up tomorrow.

The next morning, however, at breakfast time, outside Mr Parkin's back door, there was still no Ginger.

"I'm afraid that something must have happened to him," Tod's mother said sadly. And Tod's father said, "Wasn't Mr Parkin going to telephone us this evening, just to confirm that he's coming home tomorrow? What on earth are we going to say to him?"

Tod's mother just said, "Oh dear!"

That morning Tod felt very miserable. His mother was at home, and she suggested various interesting things that he might like to do; but he didn't want to do any of them. He just wandered round the garden, calling, "Ginger-ninger, where are you? Ginger-winger, come home!"

Tod knew that they'd looked into their own garden shed, but he still went there again, because there seemed nowhere else he could look. The first time he looked in, he looked very quickly, because, of course, he really knew that Ginger wasn't there. The second time he decided he must look more thoroughly, all round: at the workbench under the window; at the cupboard at the far end, where his father kept his special tools; at the garden spades and forks and hoes that hung in a row along the remaining wall. Tod even got down on all fours and looked under the lawnmower. No Ginger, of course.

That was the second time that Tod looked into the shed.

The third time he looked in, he was quietly crying to himself. It was getting dark inside the shed. He looked at the cupboard at the far end. At the bottom of the cupboard, the door fitted badly and left a gap. Suddenly, through that gap, came snaking something white – a long white furry arm.

"Ginger!" shouted Tod, and rushed to open the cupboard door; but the cupboard was kept bolted, and the bolt was too high for Tod to reach. So he ran back to the house to fetch his mother, who came hurrying at once. She unbolted the cupboard door and opened it – and out stalked Ginger!

Ginger didn't seem ill or even thin; but he did seem cross. He didn't want to be stroked or even tickled behind his ear. He went straight to the fence that separated the two gardens. He crouched at the bottom of the fence for a moment, and then with a leap he was at the top of the fence, and then over into his own garden – home!

Tod's mother fetched Mr Parkin's key and they went round to his back door. There was Ginger, his tail waving in the air, ready for his food. He had already had a long drink, they could tell, from his bowl of water. They fed him more than half a tin of cat-food, as he had missed so many meals. Then they locked up again and went home.

Later, Tod's father heard all about how Tod had found Ginger in the tool cupboard. "What a sly cat!" he said. "Yes, I remember going to that cupboard to get a tool on the very day he disappeared. I left the cupboard open for just a few minutes while I did something at the workbench. While my back was turned, he must have slipped in."

"Cats are like that," said Tod's mother.

"Anyway," said Tod's father, "we'll have something to tell old Parkin when he rings up."

Tod began jumping with excitement. "When Mr Parkin rings, can I tell him about Ginger? Can I? Can I?"

"Why not?" said his father, and looked at Tod's mother. She said, "I think Tod should tell the whole story. After all, he found Ginger. He is the hero of our desperate search."

Potlatch for Bears

A Story from Alaska

Lorle K Harris

Son-of-a-Glacier was the only living person left in the great house that was the home of the Iceberg Clan. One by one his relatives had sickened and died, wiped out by a plague that had killed so many in his village.

Son-of-a-Glacier piled driftwood in the large central hearth in the great house. He lighted the fire and watched the shadows play against the empty tier of sleeping rooms that circled the building. The silence was unbearable.

Even a lonely man has to eat, so he put a piece of halibut on a stick and roasted it over the fire. He dipped the fish into some eulachon grease and put it in his mouth. He had no appetite for food. He looked sadly at the pebbles bordering the hearth, sparkling white and pink in the reflection of the flames; but he had no eye for beauty. Life has to be shared to be enjoyed.

But how? He couldn't paddle away in search of new friends. People would think a man alone had been chased out of his village for practising witchcraft or flaunting the taboos of his tribe. He might just as well be dead.

Son-of-a-Glacier doused the fire and trudged off into the woods. He came upon a bear trail. Ah, he thought, I'll let the bears kill me; I'll lie down across the path and wait.

By and by he heard the crunch of bushes breaking under the weight of heavy feet. He looked in the direction of the sound. Sure enough, there were several grizzlies plodding along behind a giant fellow with white-tipped fur.

Cold shivers rippled over Son-of-a-Glacier's back. He didn't want the grizzlies to tear him apart. He jumped to his feet, stretched to his full height and waited. When the leader of the bears came near, Son-of-a-Glacier said, "I've come to invite you to a feast."

The huge bear's fur bristled along his back. "Man is the killer of bears."

This is the end for me, thought Son-of-a-Glacier, but he put on a brave front. "I've come to invite you to a potlatch," he repeated, "but kill me if you wish. I don't mind. I'm all alone. My wife, my children, my friends, are all dead."

The grizzly turned around. He whined to the other bears. They all turned around and disappeared into the woods.

Son-of-a-Glacier sighed with relief and hurried back to the village.

"What's the rush?" asked one of the villagers.

"I go to prepare a feast," he said. "I've invited the grizzlies to be my guests."

"Whatever made you do such a foolish thing?" asked the man. "Didn't the plague kill off enough of us? Do you want the entire village to be wiped out?" Without waiting for an answer he ran away.

He'll warn the others to lock themselves up in their houses, thought Son-of-a-Glacier.

When Son-of-a-Glacier returned to his house he removed the sooty stones from the hearth and replaced them with bright white pebbles. A potlatch called for a clean house.

Because it was a special occasion he took off his shirt and decorated his body with scarlet stripes; one over his heart, one across the upper part of his chest, and more on his upper arms.

Rising early the next morning, he took out the huge feast bowls carved of cedar logs, and filled them with berries, the fat of the eulachon fish, and three kinds of smoked salmon. Then he went outside, and stood beside the doorway to wait for his guests.

After a while he saw the giant grizzly with the white-tipped fur step out of the woods. Behind him trudged another bear, and another, and another.

The few villagers who were about hurried into their houses.

Son-of-a-Glacier ran to greet his guests, escorting them to his home. He seated the big

grizzly in the place of honour at the centre of the rear of the house. The others took their places around the walls on either side of their leader. As Son-of-a-Glacier seated each bear he called out the name of the dead man whose place he was filling.

Each bear, in turn, said, "Thank you."

Then Son-of-a-Glacier brought out the trays of cranberries and salmon and eulachon fat. The bears ate and ate and ate.

When they were finished, the giant grizzly stood up on his hind legs. He raised his right foreleg, pointing to the smoke hole above the hearth.

Gesturing with his left foreleg, like a tribal leader waving his arms as he spoke at a potlatch, he said, "The grizzlies thank Son-of-a-Glacier for a feast worthy of the Iceberg Clan. May the Clan multiply and rise again in greatness to equal the generosity of our host."

The big bear lumbered over to the doorway. "Lie down, Son-of-a-Glacier," he said.

Son-of-a-Glacier lay down. The grizzly bent over the man and licked the red stripes on his arms and breast.

"I am licking away your sorrow," he said.

Then he turned to the other bears. "Be a friend to this man. Each one of you show him your respect."

One by one the bears approached Son-of-a-Glacier and licked him. Then they left as they had come, in a single file behind their leader, the grizzly with the white-tipped fur.

And Son-of-a-Glacier was never lonely again because he had learned the way to win a friend is to be one.

The Mousewife

Rumer Godden

Wherever there is an old house with wooden floors and beams and rafters and wooden stairs and wainscots and skirting boards and larders, there are mice. They creep out on the carpets for crumbs, they whisk in and out of their holes, they run in the wainscot and between the ceiling and the floors. There are no signposts because they know the way, and no milestones because no one is there to see how they run.

In the old nursery rhyme, when the cat went to see the queen, he caught a little mouse under her chair; that was long, long ago and that queen was different from our queen, but the mouse was the same.

Mice have always been the same. There are

no fashions in mice; they do not change. If a mouse could have a portrait painted of his great-great-grandfather, and *his* great-grandfather, it would be the portrait of a mouse today.

But once there was a little mousewife who was different from the rest.

She looked the same; she had the same ears and prick nose and whiskers and dewdrop eyes; the same little bones and grey fur; the same skinny paws and long skinny tail.

She did all the things a mousewife does: she made a nest for the mouse babies she hoped to have one day; she collected crumbs of food for her husband and herself; once she bit the tops off a whole bowl of crocuses; and she played with the other mice at midnight on the attic floor.

"What more do you want?" asked her husband.

She did not know what it was she wanted, but she wanted more.

The house where these mice lived belonged to a spinster lady called Miss Barbara Wilkinson. The mice thought the house was the whole world. The garden and the wood that lay around it were as far away to them as the stars are to you, but the mousewife sometimes used to creep up on the window sill and press her whiskers close against the pane.

In spring she saw snowdrops and apple blossoms in the garden and bluebells in the wood; in summer there were roses; in autumn all the trees changed colour; and in winter they were bare until the snow came and they were white with snow.

The mousewife saw all these through the window pane, but she did not know what they were.

She was a house mouse, not a garden mouse or a field mouse; she could not go outside.

"I think about cheese," said her husband. "Why don't you think about cheese?"

Then, at Christmas, he had an attack of indigestion from eating rich crumbs of Christmas cake. "There were currants in those crumbs," said the mousewife. "They have upset you. You must go to bed and be kept warm." She decided to move the mousehole to a space behind the fender where it was warm. She lined the new hole with tufts of carpet wool and put her husband to bed wrapped in a pattern of grey flannel that Miss Wilkinson's lazy maid, Flora, had left in the dustpan. "But I am grateful to Flora," said the mousewife's husband as he settled himself comfortably in bed.

Now the mousewife had to find all the food for the family in addition to keeping the hole swept and clean.

She had no time for thinking.

While she was busy, a boy brought a dove to Miss Wilkinson. He had caught it in the wood. It was a pretty thing, a turtle-dove. Miss Wilkinson put it in a cage on the ledge of her sitting room window.

The cage was an elegant one; it had gilt bars and a door that opened if its catch was pressed down; there were small gilt trays for water and peas. Miss Wilkinson hung up a lump of sugar and a piece of fat. "There, you have everything you want," said Miss Barbara Wilkinson.

For a day or two the dove pecked at the bars and opened and shut its wings. Sometimes it called, "Roo coo, roo coo," then it was silent.

"Why won't it eat?" asked Miss Barbara Wilkinson. "Those are the very best peas."

A mouse family seldom has enough to eat. It is difficult to come by crumbs, especially in such a neat, tidy house as Miss Barbara Wilkinson's. It was the peas that first attracted the attention of the mousewife to the cage when at last she had time to go up on the window sill. "I have been running here and there and everywhere to get us food," she said, "not allowing myself to come up on to the window sill, and here are these fine peas, not to mention this piece of fat." (She did not care for the sugar.)

She squeezed through the bars of the cage, but as she was taking the first pea from the tray, the dove moved its wings. I cannot tell you how quickly the mousewife pressed herself back through the bars and jumped down from the sill and ran across the floor and whisked into her hole. It was quicker than a cat can wink its eye. (She thought it was the cat.)

In spite of her great fright she could not help thinking of those peas. She was very hungry. "I had better not go back," she said. "There is something dangerous there," but back she went the very next day.

Soon the dove grew quite used to the mousewife's going in and out, and the mouse grew quite used to the dove.

"This is better," said Miss Barbara Wilkinson. "The dove is eating its peas," but, of course, he was not; it was the mouse.

The dove kept his wings folded. The mousewife thought him large and strange and ugly with the speckles on his breast and his fine down. (She thought of it as fur, not feathers.) He was not at all like a mouse; his voice was deep and soft, quite unlike hers, which was a small, high squeaking. Most strange of all, to her, was that he let her take his peas; when she offered them to him he turned his head aside on his breast.

"Then at least take a little water," begged the mousewife, but he said he did not like water. "Only dew, dew, dew," he said.

"What is dew?" asked the mousewife.

He could not tell her what dew was, but he told her how it shines on the leaves and grass in the early morning for doves to drink. That made him think of night in the woods and of how he and his mate would come down with the first light to walk on the wet earth and peck for food, and of how, then, they would fly over the fields to other woods farther away. He told this to the mousewife too.

"What is fly?" asked the ignorant little mousewife.

"Don't you know?" asked the dove in surprise. He stretched out his wings and they hit the cage bars. Still he struggled to spread them, but the bars were too close, and he sank back on his perch and sank his head on his breast.

The mousewife was strangely moved, but she did not know why.

Because he would not eat his peas, she brought him crumbs of bread and, once, a preserved blackberry that had fallen from a tart. (But he would not eat the blackberry.)

Every day he talked to her about the world outside the window.

He told her of roofs and the tops of trees and of the rounded shapes of hills and the flat look of fields and of the mountains far away. "But I have never flown as far as that," he said, and he was quiet. He was thinking that now he never would.

To cheer him, the mousewife asked him to tell her about the wind; she heard it in the house on stormy nights, shaking the doors and windows with more noise than all the mice put together. The dove told her how it blew in the cornfields, making patterns in the corn, and of how it made different sounds in the different sorts of trees, and of how it blew up the clouds and sent them across the sky.

He told her these things as a dove would see them, as it flew, and the mousewife, who was used to creeping, felt her head growing as dizzy as if she were spinning on her tail, but all she said was, "Tell me more."

Each day the dove told her more. When she came he would lift his head and call to her, "Roo coo, roo coo," in his most gentle voice.

"Why do you spend so much time on the window sill?" asked her husband. "I do not like it. The proper place for a mousewife is in her hole or coming out for crumbs and frolic with me."

The mousewife did not answer. She looked far away.

Then, on a happy day, she had a nestful of baby mice. They were not as big as half your thumb, and they were pink and hairless, with pink shut eyes and little pink tails like threads. The mousewife loved them very much. The eldest, who was a girl, she called Flannelette, after the pattern of grey flannel. For several days she thought of nothing and no one else. She was also busy with her husband. His digestion was no better.

One afternoon he went over to the opposite wall to see a friend. He was well enough to do that, he said, but certainly not well enough to go out and look for crumbs. The mice babies were asleep, the hole was quiet, and the mousewife began to think of the dove. Presently she tucked the nest up carefully and went up on the window sill to see him;

also she was hungry and needed some peas.

What a state he was in! He was drooping and nearly exhausted because he had eaten scarcely anything while she had been away. He cowered over her with his wings and kissed her with his beak; she had not known his feathers were so soft or that his breast was so warm. "I thought you had gone, gone, gone," he said over and over again.

"Tut! Tut!" said the mousewife. "A body has other things to do. I can't be always running off to you," but though she pretended to scold him, she had a tear at the end of her whisker for the poor dove. (Mouse tears look like millet seeds, which are the smallest seeds I know.)

She stayed a long time with the dove. When she went home, I am sorry to say, her husband bit her on the ear.

That night she lay awake thinking of the dove; mice stay up a great part of the night, but, toward dawn, they, too, curl into their beds and sleep. The mousewife could not sleep. She still thought of the dove. "I cannot visit him as much as I could wish," she said.

"There is my husband, and he has never bitten me before. There are the children, and it is surprising how quickly crumbs are eaten up. And no one would believe how dirty a hole can get if it is not attended to every day. But that is not the worst of it. The dove should not be in that cage. It is thoughtless of Miss Barbara Wilkinson." She grew angry as she thought of it. "Not to be able to scamper about the floor! Not to be able to run in and out, or climb up the larder to get at the cheese! Not to flick in and out and to whisk and to feel how you run in your tail! To sit in the trap until your bones are stiff and your whiskers grow stupid because there is nothing for them to smell or hear or see!" The mousewife could only think of it as a mouse, but she could feel as the dove could feel.

Her husband and Flannelette and the other children were breathing and squeaking happily in their sleep, but the mousewife could hear her heart beating; the beats were little, like the tick of a watch, but they felt loud and disturbing to her. "I cannot sleep," said the mousewife, and then, suddenly, she felt she must go then, that minute, to the dove. "It is too late. He will be asleep," she said, but still she felt she should go.

She crept from her bed and out of the hole on to the floor by the fender. It was bright moonlight, so bright that it made her blink. It was bright as day, but a strange day, that made her head swim and her tail tremble. Her whiskers quivered this way and that, but there was no one and nothing to be seen; no sound, no movement anywhere.

She crept across the pattern of the carpet, stopping here and there on a rose or a leaf or on the scroll of the border. At last she reached the wall and ran lightly up on to the window sill and looked into the cage. In the moonlight she could see the dove sleeping in the feathers, which were ruffled up so that he looked plump and peaceful, but, as she watched, he dreamed and called "roo coo" in his sleep and shivered as if he moved. "He is dreaming of scampering and running free," said the mousewife. "Poor thing! Poor dove!"

She looked out into the garden. It too was as bright as day, but the same strange day. She could see the tops of the trees in the wood, and she knew, all at once, that was where the dove should be, in the trees and the garden and the wood.

He called "roo coo" again in his sleep – and she saw that the window was open.

Her whiskers grew still and then they stiffened. She thought of the catch on the cage door. If the catch was pressed down, the door opened.

"I shall open it," said the mousewife. "I shall jump on it and hang from it and swing from it, and it will be pressed down; the door will open and the dove can come out. He can whisk quite out of sight. Miss Barbara Wilkinson will not be able to catch him."

She jumped at the cage and caught the catch in her strong little teeth and swung. The door sprang open, waking the dove.

He was startled and lifted his wings, and they hit hard against the cage so that it shivered and the mousewife was almost shaken off.

"Hurry! Hurry!" she said through her teeth.

In a heavy sidelong way he sidled to the door and stood there looking. The mousewife would have given him a push, but she was holding down the catch.

At the door of the cage the dove stretched his neck toward the open window. "Why does he not hurry? thought the mousewife. "I cannot stay here much longer. My teeth are cracking."

He did not see her or look toward her; then – clap – he took her breath away so that she fell. He had opened his wings and flown straight out. For a moment he dipped as if he would fall, his wings were cramped, and then he moved them and lifted up and up and flew away across the tops of the trees.

The mousewife picked herself up and shook out her bones and her fur.

"So that is to fly," she said. "Now I know." She stood looking out of the window where the dove had gone.

"He has flown," she said. "Now there is no one to tell me about the hills and the corn and the clouds. I shall forget them. How shall I remember when there is no one to tell me and there are so many children and crumbs and bits of fluff to think of?" She had millet tears, not on her whiskers but in her eyes.

"Tut! Tut!" said the mousewife and blinked them away. She looked out again and saw the stars. It has been given to few mice to see the stars; so rare is it that the mousewife had not even heard of them, and when she saw them shining she thought at first they must be new brass buttons. Then she saw they were very far off, farther than the garden or the wood, beyond the farthest trees. "But not too far for me to see," she said. She knew now that they were not buttons but something far and big and strange. "But not so strange to me," she said, "for I have seen them. And I have seen them for myself," said the mousewife, "without the dove. I can see for myself," said the mousewife, and slowly, proudly, she walked back to bed.

She was back in the hole before her husband woke up, and he did not know that she had been away.

Miss Barbara Wilkinson was astonished to find the cage empty next morning and the dove gone. "Who could have let it out?" asked Miss Wilkinson. She suspected Flora and never knew that she was looking at someone too large and that it was a very small person indeed.

The mousewife is a very old lady mouse now. Her whiskers are grey and she cannot scamper any more; even her running is slow. But her great-great-grand-children, the children of the children of the children of Flannelette and Flannelette's brothers and sisters, treat her with the utmost respect.

She is a little different from them, though she looks the same. I think she knows something they do not.

ACKNOWLEDGEMENTS

The publishers wish to thank the following for permission to reproduce copyright material. All possible care has been taken to trace the ownership of every story included and to make full acknowledgement for its use. If any errors have accidentally occurred, they will be corrected in subsequent editions, provided notification is sent to the publishers.

Dick King-Smith: "A Narrow Squeak" from *A Narrow Squeak and Other Animal Stories*, by Dick King-Smith. Copyright © Fox Busters Ltd, 1993. Reproduced by permission of A P Watt Ltd

Barbee Oliver Carleton: "A Hat for Crumpet" from *A Treasury of Pony Stories*, chosen by Linda Jennings; first published by Kingfisher Books, 1996. Copyright © Highlights for Children, 1960. Reproduced by permission of Highlights for Children Inc

Michael Rosen: "The Lion and the Hare" from *The Oxfam Book of Children's Stories: South and North, East and West*, edited by Michael Rosen. Copyright © Michael Rosen, 1992, © OXFAM Activities, 1992. Reproduced by permission of Walker Books Ltd

Ursula Moray Williams: "Jeffy and Miss Amity" from *Jeffy, the Burglar's Cat* by Ursula Moray Williams; first published by Andersen Press Ltd, 1981. Copyright © Ursula Moray Williams, 1981. Reproduced by permission of Curtis Brown Ltd

A N Wilson: "The Visit of Fudge" from *Hazel the Guinea Pig* by A N Wilson. Copyright © A N Wilson, 1989. Reproduced by permission of Walker Books Ltd

Phyllis Savory: "How the Ostrich Got His Long Neck" from *The Best of African Folklore*, chosen by Phyllis Savory. Reproduced by permission of Struik Publishers (Pty) Ltd

Ruth Ainsworth: "The Flood" from *Pet Stories for Children*, edited by Sara and Stephen Corrin; first published by Faber & Faber Ltd. Reproduced by permission of Richard Gilbert

Allan Ahlberg: "The Boy Who Turned into a Dog" from *Woof!*; first published by Viking Kestrel, 1986. Copyright © Allan Ahlberg, 1986. Reproduced by permission of Penguin Books Ltd

ACKNOWLEDGEMENTS

Robin Lister: "The Lioness and the Mouse" from *A Treasury of Animal Stories*, chosen by Jane Olliver; first published by Kingfisher Books, 1992. Copyright © Grisewood & Dempsey Ltd, 1986. Reproduced by permission of Larousse plc

Colin Thompson: "Delilah the Spider" from *Sid the Mosquito*, by Colin Thompson; first published by Knight Books, 1993. Copyright © Colin Thompson 1991, 1993. Reproduced by permission of Hodder & Stoughton Ltd

David Henry Wilson: "Heaven" from *Do Gerbils Go To Heaven*? by David Henry Wilson; first published by Macmillan Children's Books, 1996. Reproduced by permission of the author

Anita Hewett: "Rabbits Go Riding" from *The Puffin Book of Animal Stories*. First published as "Honey Mouse" by The Bodley Head, 1957. Reproduced by permission of Random House UK Ltd

Dick King-Smith: The Happiest Woodlouse" from *A Narrow Squeak and Other Animal Stories*; first published 1993. Copyright © Fox Busters Ltd, 1993. Reprinted by permission of A P Watt Ltd

Philippa Pearce: "Tod and the Desperate Search" from *Here Comes Tod!* Copyright © Philippa Pearce, 1992. Reproduced by permission of Walker Books Ltd

Lorle K Harris: "Potlatch for Bears" from *Tlingit Tales: Potlatch and Totem Pole*. Copyright © Lorle K Harris 1985. Reproduced by permission of Naturegraph Publishers Inc

Rumer Godden: "The Mousewife" from *Mouse Time* by Rumer Godden; first published by Macmillan Children's Books, 1951. Reproduced by permission of Curtis Brown Ltd

Funny stories

for 7 Year Olds

Chosen by Helen Paiba

A bright and varied selection of wonderfully
entertaining stories by some of the very
best writers for children. Perfect for reading
alone or aloud – and for dipping into time
and time again. With stories from Dick
King-Smith, Michael Bond, Philippa Gregory,
Jacqueline Wilson and many more,
this book will provide hours of fantastic fun.

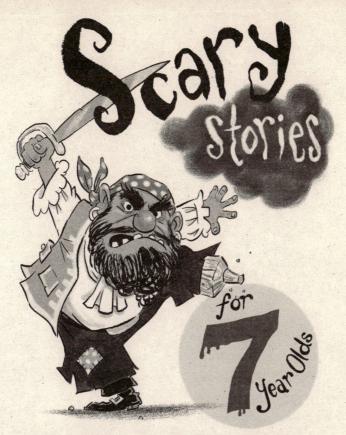

Scary stories
for 7 Year Olds

Chosen by Helen Paiba

A bright and varied selection of hair-raisingly
scary stories by some of the very best
writers for children. Perfect for reading
alone or aloud – and for dipping into time and
time again. With stories from Michael Rosen,
Catherine Storr, Jamie Rix, Rose Impey
and many more, this book will provide
hours of fantastic fun.